Three Shades of Green

Manasa Rachapalli

Published by

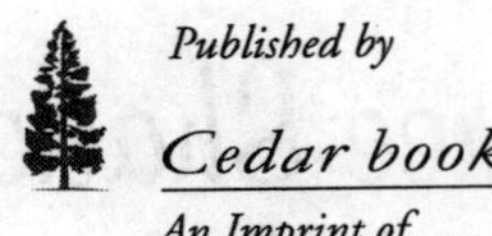

Cedar books

An Imprint of

Pustak Mahal®, **Delhi**

J-3/16 , Daryaganj, New Delhi-110002
☎ 23276539, 23272783, 23272784 • *Fax:* 011-23260518
E-mail: info@pustakmahal.com • *Website:* www.pustakmahal.com

Sales Centre

10-B, Netaji Subhash Marg, Daryaganj, New Delhi-110002
☎ 23268292, 23268293, 23279900 • *Fax:* 011-23280567
E-mail: rapidexdelhi@indiatimes.com

Branch Offices

Bangalore: ☎ 22234025
E-mail: pmblr@sancharnet.in • pustak@sancharnet.in
Mumbai: ☎ 22010941
E-mail: rapidex@bom5.vsnl.net.in
Patna: ☎ 3294193 • *Telefax:* 0612-2302719
E-mail: rapidexptn@rediffmail.com
Hyderabad: *Telefax:* 040-24737290
E-mail: pustakmahalhyd@yahoo.co.in

ISBN 978-81-223-1033-7

Edition : 2008

Printed at : Param Offsetters, Okhla, New Delhi-110020

Dedication

To Sister Clarissa, my angel and teacher,
who taught me to love words.
To my Uncle Gandhi
for convincing me to publish this book.
To Papa, Amma, and Saroo
for giving me the freedom of thought.

– Manasa Rachapalli

Contents

Preface

Three Shades of Green is a set of my first three stories coming into light. In the title, *Green* symbolises life. The stories represent different perspectives of life. Each story is completely different from the other in its setting, relationships, and emotions. All the protagonists in my stories are more human than heroes. They have mixed feelings about a particular situation in their lives that they chose impulsively or righteously. A person's life is a set of stories when the person becomes strong at one moment, weak at another moment. This book is a humble presentation of one's choices.

Sandy and Pearl, my personal favourite, involves two friends – two women facing two different problems, faced by many women in modern India. The two friends, ridiculed by family and society, face the troubles and chose a courageous path. This story is about the inner strength of a woman. Two events inspired me to write this story. One day, I heard the news of nearly twenty foetuses found in a well in a doctor's backyard, and the root cause of all this......dowry! I felt I had to do something about it all and thus the story, *Sandy and Pearl.*

The second story of the book, *A Fine Line,* in contrast to the first one is about the frailty of human nature. Today, when India is sandwiched between the western and eastern civilisation, people often do not see that there is just a fine line between fondness and real love. This story is about impulsiveness, wrong choices, and above all, betrayal, all in the name of love. Mythili is a girl working hard to make both her ends meet, who falls in love with Akash the minute she sees him. From then on, she knows her life would never be the same and thus loses herself totally to make the wrong choices. Her dreamland shatters when she finds that Akash is already engaged to be married to another girl. Even then, she stops fighting her growing feelings for him in her heart.

A year or so later, she again meets Akash, a grieving widower. She instantly builds up her hopes again and blindly she repeats the same mistake of loving him. Akash unleashes his wrath on her and overwhelmed by her grief, she takes revenge on him, in return saving herself from doom. After a few years, her past haunts her and the same sweet revenge teaches her a lesson about the fine line of love and selfishness.

The last story, *Peetam,* is a small suspense thriller filled with magic, miracles, and near personification of soul itself. The whole story revolves around a single line from Bhagavad-Gita, which describes the importance of a soul and its immortal nature. Ishwak is a seemingly normal 13-year-old until one day his parents die in a freak car accident. He is sent to his grandfather's family whom he had not seen all his life because Ishwak's parents married against his grandfather's wishes.

Strangely, when he arrives at this small sleeping village, he recognises a lot of things as if he had been there before. There are voices speaking to him and memories that were not his. In all the confusion, he finds the house packed with kids of his age and is relieved to having befriended Gita, a protégée to his grandfather in Vedas. Strange and mysterious things start happening after his arrival and Pandit Vishwanath suspects his grandson to be the cause of this destruction. He prepares himself for the dark future that hangs over his family. Ishwak slowly turns cold and plans to sacrifice Gita, his only friend! As the mystery unravels, Pandit Vishwanath understands that Ishwak is after the Peetam, a holy construction in the middle of the house that has great power. Will the grandfather save his grandson is the rest of the story.

Foreword

An unconventional story writer...

All love stories end up either as tragedies or comedies. We hardly come across stories where a lover who is heart broken befriends the breaker and continues to love him as before, not as lover now but as a friend, a well wisher, a care taker and even takes care of the child born by some other – a story, where a lover, though the love unfulfilled, becomes a sympathiser to him who breaks love, may be even if it be for compelling reasons.

We also do not so much come across stories where a friend fills in the place of almost a lover to console to such an extent that the love broken forgets the agony and the anguish as though the friend more than compensates the loss of the lover though not a lover.

Such plots make the stories different. And it is for this difference that a reader looks forward with all his eyes, ears, mind and heart open.

Though, the two love stories written here by Manasa, a very young but a very promising story writer, impressed me for that unforeseeable touch which makes a story new, novel and original.

The third piece has a surrealistic and subconscious shade- the ego and the alter ego clashing for primacy and priority, not so easily decipherable unless one has a fancy for that kind of stuff.

The stories differ from many offbeat contributions to feminist literature.

The language in the stories is very much mellowed and matured interspersed with purple patches of conversations and descriptions. In fact there are some quotable sentences like.....

"She was crying to the top of her lungs as if she knew what was ahead of her."

"A kind of shiver runs through every girl's heart when she hears her parents treat her as a guest, someone else's girl, not their own, at least not forever."

"How can I give my life away to some one I do not know and hope that he would make the right decisions for me?"

"If I give the family all they expect and do not follow my own dreams, then I will be empty, dead inside and just live for others."

"Mythili had never thought that a simple smile could be so devastatingly beautiful."

"What is a sunflower without a sun?"

"Sheshadri has a foul mind matching his foul breath."

"Her dark eyelashes were like a painter's strokes that moved swiftly whenever she blinked and she blinked so often."

"There were too many questions and no answers."

"It was a beautiful sight, more beautiful than the sun."

"She always felt it was too good to be true."

"The front yard of the railway station was like a twist in the story."

"Like a tide of waves washing the lines on the sand, something cleansed those memories away."

"She could not even love herself without his love."

"A telegram never brings good news, his experience told him. The post man with a letter is always appreciated than the post man with a telegram."

which speak of the literary flourish and finish of the author, which are of high order considering her age and experience.

I don't think I should go into too many details of telling what, why, and how of them, which would amount to something like telling about a cinema to some one even before he sees it. That conditions him to look at it with a preconceived angle. A writer of an Intro should not destroy the mystery of a story or a novel or a poem by over dilating on it except by touching on the vision and the philosophy and the excellent expressions, which make them "literature".

I congratulate the author for her control and composure in converting what the "real" might have been into the "ideal". There is a message and a mission in them to the modern lovers not to confuse fashion for passion, liking for loving.

– D.V. Kondala Rao
Honorary Chairman
Viswanatha Sahitya Peetham
Editor- Jayanthi, bilingual.

1

Sandy and Pearl

THERE IS NOTHING sweeter than the voices of two little girls playing with sand on seashore along with the orchestra of sea itself.

"Come let's make a house for us to stay together in it when we are cross with our parents," called Sneha looking at her dearest friend, Sandhya. She loved her curly hair that would jog along whenever she moved, she liked watching her curls jump when she walked, when she ran, or when she talked about how she would travel the world the way her uncle did. But Sandy did not like them (Sandhya would insist Sneha calling her Sandy). She hated her curls because mom always had a tough time combing her hair, so she would comb her really hard that it hurt. She always tangled them, they were a mess. She would cover them up with a hat.

"Yes, I'm coming." Sandy turned around, a little disgusted. Sneha bugged her sometimes. She always wanted her to sit and play and make things like houses and dolls. But she loved running around, chasing the waves, finding crabs and teasing them. She hoped she would find pearls in the water and become rich. She secretly hoped she would find a black pearl. She had been in love with black pearls ever since her uncle told her a story of treasure hunt and how everyone was searching for a black pearl that had magical powers. If she found it then she would take Sneha with her, away from her parents, chuckled Sandy. Sandy hated Sneha's parents for they always scolded her and shouted at her. Everything she did was wrong in their view.

"Sneha, I decided to change your name." informed Sandy while helping her build a house out of sand.

"What! How can you change my name? My name is beautiful. I don't want to change it to any other name."

"I will not hear anything you say. I am Sandy and you should have a cool name like that. I decided to call you 'Pearl'. Don't you like that name? It's so beautiful."

"Pearl, hmm…it sounds cool. I like it. But only you can call me Pearl. Is that a deal?"

"Oh no, no one would dare call you Pearl other than me."

Laughing, both the girls bonded a little closer every minute that passed by.

"Look! We made such a beautiful house. I wish we could become small and live in it. Wouldn't it be wonderful, just like Lilliputs?" cried Sandy.

"Yes, that would be great! But I have to get back home by evening otherwise I will get a good scold from my mom and she will ask me to leave the house," Sneha frowned.

"Then you come and live with me. There is plenty of room in my room. We can share my bed. You can read my books and play with my toys, except Elmo, that's my favourite toy. I cannot give it to you. We can also share my parents," laughed Sandy.

"I will come to your house only if you give me your Elmo," teased Sneha. Annoyed, Sandy ran after Sneha to catch her, but Sneha ran away laughing.

The laughter echoed in Pearl's heart. She sighed at the joy and innocence of her childhood. The words of Sandy were her only hope now… "You can come and live with me." Holding her sari *pallu* closer to make her warm, she stared out of the window of the red bus' sill into the darkness that engulfed her.

✧

FLASH NEWS. . . . FLASH News. . . . **Flash** News. . . . . **Flash** News Rolled on the bottom of the television. The news channel would not let anyone miss out what they had to say. Sneha hurried into a crampy complex, where she worked. But something made her freeze. Suddenly her heart skipped a beat and a sweat drop crawled its way down on her brow. She turned her head to her left side and saw the TV shop. She slowly walked towards the TV as if she saw a ghost. She stared at the screen beyond the glass case. She put her hand on the glass to support herself.

The confident lady reporter with a mike in her hands and a look of scorn on her face stood in front of a supposedly normal-looking well.

"Yesterday by accident this well was discovered, which is the evidence of the monstrous side of the so-called great Indian culture. About fifteen baby dead bodies, all of which were females, were removed from this well. The police are further investigating on who must have dumped these babies in the well and were they alive when they were dumped here. The ages of the babies varies from foetus to two days old. But it remains an open secret that these are the acts of the parents who cannot afford a handsome dowry for their girls. Though dowry has become illegal in India, it still remains the evil that has rooted so deep in Indian soil that not only innocent women, even babies are sacrificed to quench its thirst. We will bring more exclusive reports on 'the well of horror'. Please stay tuned. . . . ."

The words of the reporter fainted away as Sneha felt her whole body go numb. Tears rolled down her cheeks and she felt her heart beat so fast as if it wanted to get out of her chest and cry out to the world, her woes, her pain, and her anger towards people who do not care or raise voices against such animosity.

She could not go further. She could not go and work today. She needed to find a secure place and calm down for a while. Wiping her tears off of her cheek, she went to a nearby STD shop that was announcing its presence with its yellow colour. She called up her office, "Hello, is it Sarada? Yes hi! I want to take a day off. Oh no, nothing is wrong with me. I am just not feeling well. No, I am not crying; it's just that I have a cold, so I am sounding like that to you. Ok bye, just cover for me ok. Bye. See you tomorrow."

It took all her strength to make that phone call. She could not bear to see anyone now. She did not even have the strength to stand up. She called an auto that was passing by; "Akhil Park" was all that she could say to the auto driver. When she reached her house, annoyed with the auto driver's constant puzzled looks into the mirror, she gave him the money on the meter and ran away saying, "Keep the change." Her hands were shivering as she opened the lock and all she could do was to go in, lock the door behind her, and collapse into the *Deewaan* and cry as aloud as she could, so that her heart would not burst open.

"Hello. Sandy how are you? It's been long since we met." The raspy voice of Sarada always brought a smile on Sandy's face.

"Nothing can happen to a devil. You know I will always be fine. Yes, it's been ages since we met. We should all meet someday, for a ladies day out or something like that. We will do that next weekend. Deal?"

"Commanding like always, I love it when you command such sweet things. Yes, that's a deal," giggled Sarada.

"Good."

"But listen. I called you to ask about Sneha. Is she alright? Did something happen that would upset her?"

"Pearl! She was fine when she left for office today. What happened?"

"Are you sure she was fine? She took the day off. She said she was not feeling well because of cold. She sounded upset to me. I just called up to ask if you knew anything about this."

"Oh! I don't know what happened. I will check on her. Thanks for telling me this, Sarada. I will get back to you when I talk to her."

"No problem Sandy. I know how shy Sneha is. She would only talk to you if she has any problem. You have always been kind of an elder sister to her. Take care. Bye."

"Bye. You also take care." Saying that, she pushed the end button habitually. She was concerned what could have happened that would upset Sneha.

Sandy recalled that it's been more than a year since Sneha had come to her door suddenly, shivering like a new born fawn. She could never forget that desperate look in her eyes and how she hugged her and cried like a baby. She said she lost her child and wanted to be away for a little while from her family. When Sneha calmed down a bit, she said "do you remember when we were kids, you said that I can come and live with you? So hear I am." She laughed and her laughter was filled with emptiness and fear. Without a moment's hesitation, Sandy assured her "What are friends for?"

Though Sandy found her friend to be strange at the beginning, Sneha slowly recouped and she was glad that Sneha was living with her because Sandy lived alone and away from family, and Sneha filled that gap. Once or twice she asked if her husband knew that Sneha was living with her, but Sneha said the marriage was over and she would never go back to him again. Sandy thought it was only temporary and that once she was normal again, she would think more clearly and she would resume her life. But after nearly a year, she knew that Sneha was never going back to her life again. She knew there was some strong reason for her to be acting this way, but she waited for Sneha to get the strength to talk about it.

Coming back from her thoughts, Sandy felt Sneha must have gone home. She called the landline, it was ringing, but she was not lifting it. After two calls, Sneha lifted the phone, "Hello" she sounded weak.

"Pearl! What happened? You sound awful. Is everything alright?"

"Nothing's wrong, I am fine."

"Do you want me to come home?"

"No need for that, I am fine."

"Sarada called asking me if you were alright. I thought you went to the office. What happened, why did you come back?"

"I got a terrible headache. That's the reason I came home…... When will you be back Sandy?"

"The usual timing, eight o'clock, but I will try to come soon today. Just take rest. I will be there as soon as possible."

Sneha smiled, "Ok, that will be good."

BUT SANDY CAME home the same time as everyday. Sandy grumbled at her boss for not letting her go home even an hour early, "Gadidha vedhava! Eppudoo overaction chestadu." She sighed with relief when she reached home at last. She pushed the calling bell and as the door opened, she was shocked to see the ghostly person that stood before her.

"Pearl! What happened? What's wrong? Have you been crying?"

"Oh Sandy!" Sneha hugged her crying, "My baby, my baby is not alone. She is with those other babies. She is not alone."

"Your baby is not alone. What are you talking about? Who are the other babies?" She took the sobbing Sneha to the Deewan and made her sit, where she collapsed. "Just lie down here; I will come back in a moment. Don't cry Pearl, I'm here with you. Everything will be fine. Don't cry. I will just be back. I will prepare some tea for you."

In a hurry, Sandy prepared tea and took a towel, put it under a pump and came back to Sneha. She was still crying. Sandy put her hand on her friend's shoulder lovingly and said, "Pearl, don't cry dear. Just get up." She wiped her face with the wet towel and then gave her the tea, Sneha turned it away, but Sandy persisted, "Drink it, you will feel better and then you can start telling me what is bothering you. Come on, drink it." Reluctantly, Sneha emptied the cup. "Ok, now tell me what happened? Why are you so upset?"

Sneha looked into her friend's concerned, but reassuring eyes, "Did you see today's news?"

"Yes, but I did not see anything particular except a horrifying news of the discovery of a well, the media calls it the 'well of horror'. Babies were found in it. But, what's that got to do with you?"

Sneha burst into a cry again, "My baby faced the same injustice those babies faced, Sandy. My baby, my life, is with those babies in heaven."

Sandy was shocked to hear this, "WHAT?"

"I wish I was with my baby, Sandy. It's not right. She was so young; she is supposed to be with me, not with other babies. Sandy……I want my baby back." Sneha sniffed.

Sandy was still in shock. All she could do was, hug her Pearl closer and gently pat her back. Sandy could not hold her tears back when she fully understood what was going on.

"I could not protect my baby, Sandy. I am the reason why my baby is dead. I could not protect my baby." Sneha was uncontrollably crying.

"Shhh…shhh…Don't say that. You have done nothing wrong. Now you have cried all day long and you are not feeling good. I just want you to sleep for now. Just sleep. You can tell me everything about it in the morning my Pearl." Sandy cradled her mourning friend to sleep. She let her sleep for sometime and then she prepared some hot coffee and sat by her side looking at her friend's swollen face. Her cheeks were still wet with her tears. She dried them with a cloth and looked at her. She looked tired.

She remembered the day when Sneha got engaged, she had never seen such a beautiful girl. She was happy for her friend. She hoped the best for her that day and that she would be always this happy all her life. Sandy went back in time, where everything was filled with hope, everything was beautiful, and the future seemed promising. Every girl dreams of getting married to a man who would love her and protect her. Sandy and Sneha were not different. They told each other every possible detail that they thought or dreamt; how they were going to spend their lives and how their homes would be like. Sandy wanted to explore the world as a kid, but as she grew up, she became practical and knew her middle class finances would not allow what she wanted. She thought she would do hard work and get good grades in whatever she does and do a job, get married to a guy that her father chose for her and live her life to the fullest, no matter what.

Sneha did not have much of options of education or a job. Her parents were typical middle class orthodox family and she was brought up in the system, where a girl would always be a second priority, may it be in clothes, education, or needs. She was made aware at a young age that she was to go to another home of her own (in-laws) and that her birth home was not her permanent home. She is to serve another family, look after the family and place their needs in priority to her needs and wants. She was trained not to complain so that she would please everyone in the in-laws' house. Everything she did was judged according to how she should behave in the future in-laws' house. She was also trained in such a way as to please her husband in every possible way. She was taught how to cook, stitch, look after the house, and all other household things. Though she stopped going to school at an early age, she was smart and learnt embroidery and she did such excellent embroidery that all the women in the neighbourhood would get embroidery done on their saris and give her good amount of money for the work, but she was too modest to take the money.

Sandy always teased Sneha that she was a robot to listen to all what her parents had to say, but she knew Sneha was a very sweet girl and that any man who would marry Sneha would be lucky. Sneha was engaged at a very young age of 17 and married to Satish Kumar, a clerk in the nearby village. Sandy was very sad when she knew Sneha was leaving the village to go to another village, to live with her in-laws. Sandy always hated the elders saying that the sooner a girl is married, the better off the family and the girl are. The elders in the village came and advised Sandy's father to get her married too. Too much of education for a girl would only ruin her they used to say, but Sandy's father knew it was not so. He wanted Sandy to read and if possible do a good job so that he can get her married to an educated person in the city than let her stay in a village. Sandy loved her father for his conviction and thought she would never fail her father.

Sneha presented Sandy with a sari she worked embroidery on the occasion of her marriage. It was the best work of Sneha till then. It was a pink sari with silver thread work, rich with silver and pearl beads on the border of the sari. The sari had made heads turn. Sandy wore the sari at the wedding. Everyone was praising, how beautiful she looked in that sari. Sneha had mixed emotions that day. She was jubilantly happy and anxious at the same time. How she teased her.

Sandy's memories dissolved, Sneha was still sleeping. She went in and opened the cupboard and took out the sari. The sari really was a timeless piece. She sighed as she remembered how she was crying when Sneha was leaving at the end of the wedding day for her in-laws' house. Both hugged and cried for a long time. Everyone joked that Sandy should find a suitable groom in the same place, where Sneha was going to live. She was irritated of those jokes even now. She prepared the bed beside the *Deewan* so that she would be by her side if Sneha awoke in the middle of the night. She stroked Sneha's head and settled on the bed aside to sleep. She did not know how to console her the next day. She prayed to God and slipped into dreams.

✧

THE NEXT MORNING, Sandy woke earlier than usual, just in case. Pearl was still sleeping. She set to work that instant. She prepared Pearl's favourite dish of Poori with Tomato curry. She prepared the South Indian coffee decoction so as to mix with milk and prepare the excellent coffee that Pearl always liked. She had breakfast and called up her boss to ask for a leave. He did not agree at first, but at last he gave the leave. She switched off the phone. She sat beside Pearl, anxiously waiting for her to wake up.

Sneha opened her heavy eyes, she wondered for a moment where she was. She felt scared. But then sitting in front of her, reading a book, she saw Sandy and felt secure again.

"Hi Sandy Mandy," she smiled as Sandy turned to look at her with smiling surprise.

"Don't call me Mandy, you hippo!" Sandy smiled and naughtily lifted her eyebrows. "How is my Pearl this morning?" Sandy's brow folded with concern.

"I am fine. I am sorry; I must have frightened you yesterday. I saw the news and I lost control."

"Sorry would not do," Sandy shook her head. "You scared me, the punishment for that would be for you to eat my Pooris," Sandy laughed aloud when she saw the surprised look on Sneha's face.

"Oh my God! Really! Not that punishment, anything but that."

"Enough of the jokes now; just go and get ready. You did not have your dinner yesterday," saying that Sandy pulled Sneha from the bed and pushed her in the direction of the bathroom.

"Ok *baba*, I am going. No need to push me as if I were in gallows," hurried Sneha tying her hair up.

When Sneha freshened up and was back, Sandy arranged the plates and was waiting for her near the dinner table.

"Sandy...about yesterday...," Sneha was about to say something, when Sandy stopped her, "first eat something, we can talk later."

When they finished the breakfast, Sneha licked her fingers, “that was the most fantastic breakfast ever.”

Sandy smiled, “Thanks, see I give very good punishments.”

When they finished washing the dishes and arranging them back in the rack, Sandy called “Sneha”.

Sneha felt a stir when Sandy called her by her name, she never calls her by her real name unless she really wanted to talk something serious, “Yes, ask me.”

Sandy hesitated but she had to ask, “What happened to the baby? You need not tell me if you cannot talk about it.”

Sneha took a deep breath, her eyes seemed to become moist again, “I don’t know how to say it. The day I reached my in-laws’ home, I had no bounds to my happiness; I instantly fell in love with Satish Kumar (That name seemed so alien to her now!). I thought I reached my destiny. Now I could belong to someone and that he would take care of me in every way. But on my first night at my in-laws’ house, I knew my life was not going to be the way I dreamed it to be.”

Sneha seemed to be lost in her thoughts for a moment. “But I accepted it to be my fate,” she closed her eyes hard for a minute as if it hurt even to talk about fate. “I tried to see my mother-in-law and father-in-law as my own parents and their every command was fulfilled. It did not bother me much. My only friend there was my sister-in-law, Pallavi whom we called ‘Sweety’. She was a bit naughty, and she made me laugh if she saw me I was not in good mood. She was just like my sister, but she could not be very free in front of my mother-in-law. Nothing seemed to be difficult, except my relation with my husband. It seemed that my only relation with him was that of a servant to him. He ordered things around, both socially and intimately, but would never talk heart to heart. I felt lonely sometimes, but I thought with time we would become closer. I was still filled with hope. He might one day ‘love’ me. I thought if we would have children then we would grow in love and then he would care about me. With that one hope, my days passed on and then one day I was not feeling well, something stirred in my stomach, and then I knew I was becoming a 'mother', I just felt it. And the doctor said I was right! I thought now everything will be fine. When I told my mother-in-law that I was pregnant, she was surprised pleasantly. She proudly said, "It's going to be a boy! I just know it. It is going to be a boy. We will have an heir for our family. A million thanks to the graceful God."

I was concerned when she said she was sure that it was going to be a boy. I asked her, "it would be great if it is a boy, but it will also be great if it is a girl, a girl is the omen of Goddess Lakshmi coming into the house, isn't she? I saw pure rage and a shade of hate in my mother-in-law's eyes, "SHUT UP," she said in a stern warning tone. I was shocked to see my mother-in-law like that.

I was scared. I felt very insecure and started getting tensed. One night I went to Satish. I wanted to burst out into a cry, I just stood there by the side of the cot, where he lied down after changing into his comfortable white pajamas that he liked very much.

"Mother told me about the good news," Satish looked up at me, probably for the first time in my life; he looked at me with respect. He climbed down the bed and came towards me, looked right into me and kissed me on my forehead. My heart skipped a beat, tears rolled down my eyes. "Why, what happened, are you feeling well? You should be taking care of yourself now, I don't want anything to happen to you or our baby," he smiled proudly.

"It's nothing, I am just happy," I lied.

Satish smiled, "That's good." He again went back to the bed and was about to settle down to sleep. I had to say something; I had to know what he felt.

"*Athayya* said something today that made me think she did not want a baby girl; I think she is very much attached to the idea of a baby boy. She may not accept a baby girl." I heard Satish sigh disapprovingly. I did not stop there, "What do 'you' think?"

"Don't worry; it won't be a girl, it will be a boy. It has always been that way in our family. There is always a boy first. We are going to have a baby boy. My mom is always right. Don't think unnecessarily. Go to sleep," he said with a stern voice.

"Sandy……that was the last day of my happiness. The days went uneventful. Satish though was a little excited at first, slowly became his usual self. He did not care much. And my mother-in-law would always talk about 'the baby boy' that would make me nervous."

"I was one week less of completing nine months, when I felt sharp pain in my stomach. I could not take it. I felt I could not handle the pain. I was taken to the hospital and the doctors said they had to do a C-section. My blood was very less and they had to give me a blood transfusion. And after the operation, at last I heard the voice Sandy, that sweet angelic voice I can never forget. My baby was crying. The doctor said it was a 'girl'. She was crying at the top of her lungs as if she knew what was ahead of her. I saw her for the first time and I fell in love with her, if you saw her Sandy, you would have also fallen in love with her," Sneha's eyes glistened.

"Yes I would, surely I would my Pearl," now Sandy was scarily guessing what might have happened next.

"I lost a lot of blood. So they gave me something that made me sleep for half of the day. When I woke up, I knew something inside me was empty, I felt something terrible had happened. I called out for my nurse, "Sister, where is my baby? I want to see my baby."

The nurse said she would call my husband and went away. I knew she was hiding something; Satish came in a few minutes later. He sat beside me, looking at the wall in front of him. I caught his shirt, "Satish where is my baby? Where is my 'Chitti'?" Satish still did not talk and he was turning his head away, he looked ill, "Why are you not talking? Look at me," I said firmly, "Where is my baby?"

"She is dead!" Satish said it in a slightly raised tone and looked at me for a brief moment and then looked away. I felt dizzy. Satish continued, "You lost a lot of blood and the baby could not survive. She died right after you fell asleep. I am just coming from the burial ground where I buried her. I knew you could not take it. So I did not show the dead body to you. You could not have seen her."

"Each of his answers came as a stab deep into my stomach, each one harder than the one before. I do not know Sandy, for how long I cried or I was lost. I just did not know what I would do without my Chitti. I thought of you all the time Sandy. I didn't have anyone to talk to. I didn't feel like talking to my parents or my in-laws. I just wanted to be with you. I thought only you would understand my pain Sandy." Sneha started crying again.

"No Pearl, don't cry, my Pearl. Oh! I feel so ashamed now; I was so lost in my own problems that I did not care what was going on with my friend's life. I am so sorry." Sandy could not see her friend's tears anymore. "I am really sorry."

"I needed you Sandy so badly, where were you at that time? I wrote so many letters, why didn't you answer them?" questioned Sneha with her watery eyes looking directly at Sandy.

"What letters? I did not get any letters. I knew that you had a baby but she died. I did not get any letters. But I am sorry Pearl, even though I knew it, I could not come." Sandy felt the pang of guilt hit her hard.

"Look at my fate, I could not even turn to my friend to be consoled. But I had to face something more gruesome after that. One day, when I woke up in the middle of the night, I felt thirsty and I went to the kitchen to get some water. I heard some voices that were muffled and very fast. First it was inaudible, but then I recognised the voices, they were that of Satish and my sister-in-law who had returned just that day from our relative's house in the neighbouring village. They seemed to be arguing about something. I tried to listen to what they were talking about. I was just one week out from the hospital and I was still feeling the pain around my stitches and I was still weak.

"What have you done Satish? How could you do it?"

"I need not explain anything to you Sweety. You are my younger sister; you are being out of your limits talking to your elder brother like that. Where are your manners?"

"Where are my manners? You are talking about my manners? This is ridiculous! Where is your humanity? Where is the father in you? How could you do this to your own child?"

"I know what I did; I did what is best for the family. And you better keep your mouth shut," warned Satish.

"How could you do it brother? I am ashamed to call you my brother, how could you kill your own child? And how could have mother be alright with this?"

Sandy, I can still see them talking about my baby, my sister-in-law and my husband. I knew then something sinister has happened to my Chitti, and that her own father has killed her. My head was spinning and I just collapsed then and there. The next day I woke up. Sweety sat beside me. She hugged me, but I did not cry. These people meant nothing to me then. I had to run away from there. I could not go to my parent's house. They would again bring me back here, saying once a girl is married, she is to stay at her husband's house, no matter what. I took out my jewels, some money and I felt the only place I could stay, was with you Sandy. There was no place for me anywhere else in the world. I came running, I ran away from that place of killers, ran away from my Chitti's killers, ran away from my cowardly self, I ran away as fast as I could, never looking back even once. But I could not save my little girl, my Chitti. I am also responsible for her death Sandy," Sneha burst into tears.

"Pearl! Don't say that. You are not responsible for it. You have got to be strong."

"When I heard the news about the well that was discovered, all these memories came back to me that I wanted to bury for so long. And it all came back to me again, the guilt, the disgust, the hatred, everything came back. Sometimes I wish I had the courage to go back to the village and kill everyone responsible for her death. But what will I do with myself? I am also responsible for her death. What should I do with myself? Kill myself? I could not do that."

"Pearl, my Pearl, don't talk like that. Everything will be fine. Don't worry, everything will be fine," she hugged her Pearl.

✧

MERE NASEEB MEIN tu hai ki nahi, tere naseeb mein mai huin ki nahi. . .

A song about two lovers' fate went on in the old radio in the shop adjacent to their house. It's been a few days since the truth came out. Sandy smiled at the song. Love songs, movies, everything seemed so lifeless and colourless now. She felt sick to her stomach when she thought that in some families, people that we love are willing to kill their own children just because of the gender or just because they could not pay dowry, and it being so common in our country. Slowly, like everything else in life, the effect wore off. She had to accept that the society was not perfect. We cannot wait for a modern Raja Ram Mohan Roy to come to the rescue and fight the atrocities of modern India. To make something right in our life, only we have the power to do it. But all Sandy could do right now was to take care of Pearl, take care that she was not alone in what she was going through. But she was hurt a bit and she was also ashamed about something Sneha had said to her.

"I needed you Sandy so badly, where were you at that time?"

There was a simple answer to that question and yet it was not so simple. She could have been with her if she wanted to. But she was lost in her own world at that time. She was really lost.

It has been more than a year, she thought, it must be around when Sneha was in her sixth month of pregnancy. She was about to complete her final year of degree. She had high hopes of what she was about to do. She wanted to go to the city and find a job, a good job and live her life on her own terms. Her parents have suffered to financially support her. She wanted to make them proud; moreover she wanted to be proud of herself. But then, she could remember the day when her heart sank when her father was talking about getting her married. Some old friend of his had brought a match for her.

"Sandhya is lucky to have this match. The father of Prakash Aleti, the bridegroom, is a respectable man in the city. They wanted a girl who was a bit educated for their son who is a bank manager and they liked our pretty Sandhya as soon as they saw her photo. I always knew Sandhya was a lucky girl. She would rule in her in-laws' house," Sandy overheard her father talking to her mother.

She saw her dreams crashing down. But she thought over the situation and thought the positive side of it. She still had some hope. She knew the man lived in the city. She would be able to read in a better university or do a job in a better office. She felt excited about her idea. She decided to ask about this, her mother would be the right person to talk to.

Anxious in her heart, she remembers with contempt that she was about to beg her own right to choose her life, she approached her mother who was folding some clothes, "*Amma*, you are looking really beautiful today. I hope I would look like you when I am your age." Her mother laughed, "*Donga*, you say such wonderful lies. What do you want? There must be something that you want from me. Now go on, ask me, now you will be a few days guest in our house," her mom smiled with a kind of sadness in her eyes.

"Guest for a few days? Don't say that *Amma*, I was born here and this is my real home," cried out Sandy and her eyes were suddenly wet.

A kind of shiver runs through every girl's heart when she hears her parents treat her as a guest, someone else's girl, not their own, at least not forever. I don't know about the rest of the world, but in India, a girl does not totally belong to either her parent's or her in-laws'. She is '*Adapilla*,' (Their daughter, both to birth place and in-laws' place). She does not belong to her parents completely as they think she is to leave for her in-laws' house, and equally she does not belong to the in-laws' house because she has come from a different family. She smiled sardonically. She hated that word.

"*Amma*, what will happen to my studies?" Seeing her mom perplexed, she said, "I mean my studies should be of some value, isn't it? I can't just become a housewife after putting so much hard work all these years studying." Sandy searched for positive answer in her mom's eyes. Her mom did not see her eye to eye. She continued folding her sari. Sandy could see her brow filled with care, "What happened? Tell me *Amma* that I can read further or at least work in the future."

Her mom sighed, she put the sari down after folding it and sat on the bed, "My child, my love, from now on your fate rests upon your in-laws, especially your husband."

Hearing this, Sandy felt her dreams sinking in the quicksand. She knew that this happened to all her friends who were married earlier than her, but she never thought she would be one of them. She always thought her life was going to be different.

Seeing her daughter's ghastly face, her mom added, "Sandhya, it is better you see the reality and accept it. If you do not accept it, you will only suffer, but still the consequence would be the same. Accept it and do your duty, then you would be much happier."

Sandy was angry at this, "What if I don't want to be 'much happier'? I want to be the 'happiest person' and that too on my own terms. How can I give my life away to someone I do not know and hope that he would make the right decisions for me?" She almost lost her temper.

"Sandhya! Where are your manners? Have you only learnt to be arrogant with elders? Haven't I taught you anything? If everyone starts losing their temper whenever the situation in life is not going according to their plans then no one would be happy in this world". Seeing her daughter sulk, she calmed down, "See Sandhya, we are your parents; we are not your enemies. We would choose the best for your future. But this is the best we could do for you. How you mould your life is up to you. And who knows may be Prakash would let you read or do a job. It may take time for both of you to understand each other and when he understands that your happiness lies in that, he would certainly do what is best for you both. Have some faith my little Sandhya. Now cheer up." Her mother affectionately ran down her hand on Sandy's head. "Don't think too much. Now I need to go, I have to cook lunch."

Sandy looked at her mother hurrying off to the cramped kitchen. Her mother looked tired. All her life she has accepted every trial, from financial troubles to emotional troubles. She has been an excellent house wife, an excellent mother, but she has exhausted herself serving others she loved, she had no time for herself. She would not ask anything for herself. Her only entertainment was the radio that plays old melodies while she worked. She thought, "if *Amma* could do it then I can do it, I am her daughter." But a voice inside her whispered, "You are not your mother."

The elders had decided that the engagement and marriage would have one month gap and the auspicious dates were set for the two events. As the day of engagement approached, relatives started pouring in. Everyone had their say about the marriage. Some said she was lucky, some said the guy looked very handsome, some gave advices on how to behave in the in-laws' house. Sandy always wondered if the guy was also given so many advices as to how to behave with his wife and with his in-laws.

She thought she was getting adjusted to the idea of marriage and her future, when one day one of her aunts came from the neighbouring village, her father's sister, who Sandy had already given the title of being the most obnoxious person she had ever met. Her aunt caught her hand and while examining the jewellery she was wearing, asked, "Sandy how much dowry is your father willing to give to your banker husband? I heard your in-laws are very strict about it. They want half of the money on the engagement day it seems. And, moreover, they want a motor bike and some gold jewellery, it seems. Has your father arranged for everything, otherwise we will not be able to walk in the society with our heads up."

Sandy did not think about this very seriously. But she was disgusted when her aunt said that if the dowry was not given they would not be able to walk with dignity in the society. What was wrong with the society, the dowry which is legally banned seems to have become a status symbol and the victims had no right to complain! That was absurd. Why is this system persisting in the great culture of India? She had to ask her father about this. She waited for the right time. Her father was in the best of the mood when he was having coffee in the morning, reading the newspaper.

She tiptoed to her father's side, "*Nanna*, can I ask you something?"

Her father saw Sandy, smiled, removed the glasses, folded the newspaper and said "Ask me anything my baby. When you get married, may be we will not be able to talk for long on world affairs or make fun of movies together."

"*Nanna*, don't say like that, even if I get married and have kids, even if I get old, I will always have time for you," Sandy frowned, no one was going to let her forget that she was to leave her house permanently. "I wanted to talk to you about the dowry. How much are they asking for, *Nanna*?

"Don't fret yourself in these issues. You are a kid, no need to storm your mind on all these matters. Just enjoy yourself. Ask anything else you want, a good silk sari, jewellery, anything my child," her father avoided the topic.

"I have heard they wanted half of the dowry on the engagement day strictly. Is that true? It seems a strange request *Nanna*." She saw her father's forehead frown, but she continued, "Also, added to the dowry, I heard they want a bike and some jewellery too. Is it true *Nanna*?"

Her father could not avoid his daughter's anxious questions, "Yes darling, they are asking all that, but I am giving this all to you, you rightfully deserve them. I am not giving these things to anyone else; I am giving it to you so that you could be happy. It is not something out of my budget; I always thought I would give these to you when you get married."

"If you are giving everything to me then what is my future husband giving me *Nanna*? And how can this be in your budget? I know this is not affordable for you. Along with this dowry, you will have the expenses of the marriage too. You will be in debt *Nanna*. It feels weird, as if this is not meant to happen. It also seems weird that they are asking half the dowry before engagement. Dowry has become illegal, but we are still giving it," she had now said too much. She saw anger in her father's eyes. She knew she had upset him too much.

"Sandhya!" her father said with anger in his tone, but trying to suppress it, "We live in a real world. A marriage without dowry is only theoretical and unpractical in society. And if I give some money to my son-in-law to take care of my daughter as a present then it is not a big crime. This is just a father's gift to his daughter. Do not think too much over these issues. Moreover, just your thinking or my thinking does not change the world. Right now, just concentrate on your studies and get 1st class for graduation."

"But *Nanna*......"

"Sandhya, let me do my duty as a father. Don't worry too much about these things. You will be happy in this family, I assure you. I would not want to talk much about this."

Sandy understood her father would not listen to her or her concerns. He could not answer them because he had no answers himself. Sandy felt 'we are all slaves to the invisible system of culture of beliefs about daughters and dowry'. She could not fight her own father. She could not dare to hurt him. For some reason, her father seems to think that Prakash would keep her happy. Finally, she let go off her thoughts. I would do anything for my parents. I have to accept things the way they are. Again, a small voice inside her whispered a little louder, 'you are capable of doing more. Don't lose.' But Sandy went on with her life, going to college, reading, and getting ready for exams, little did she knew that her world would turn upside down in a few days and she would hurt her parents beyond her imagination.

Her engagement was a small ceremony in her house. All her relatives were present, her future relatives came to their house, and she saw her "would be" for the first time. He was a handsome guy and looked as an honest person. She liked him. Even Prakash caught Sandy looking at him once or twice and smiled at her teasingly. But…there was this 'but' coming in her mind all the time, he would not be here if my father would not have given him the money he wanted. She never understood how one of the most important relationships in life is based on money. Her heart troubled her. But she felt that some things in life should be compromised, she had to do this at least for her parents. She did not want to trouble them; they will face ridicule in the society if she did anything stupid.

One day, Prakash wanted to talk to her; as she was already engaged to him, Sandy's parents agreed that he can talk to her. But the meeting was to take place in the backyard of Sandy's house. Sandy thought this was her opportunity to set things right or at least know what her future held for her. She was nervous, she thought over what to ask him and how to ask him.

Prakash came in the next day. Two chairs were arranged in the backyard underneath the mango tree. It was the end of August; rains did an excellent job to build an air of romance in the humble backyard. Sandy's rose garden was at its full bloom with vibrant colours of red and pink, with a touch of white roses. The fragrance could make anyone realise that heaven was right here on earth.

"Beautiful garden, your father said that you take care of this garden and you know a lot about plants, especially flowering plants."

Sandy could see that even Prakash was tensed about this meeting, she answered 'yes.'

Prakash smiled, "And I don't think you buy any mangoes in summer, you have quite a big tree right here, I guess it gives you good amount of mangoes for the summer."

Sandy proudly answered, "Yes, the best mangoes; in fact our neighbours cannot resist when the tree is at its fullest bloom, we send some out to them. May be the coming summer you can also have some, you will really enjoy them." Sandy suddenly felt shy.

"I would really like that," Sandy could see Prakash's eyes sparkle. Prakash went on, "the reason I wanted to talk to you was to know you a bit better, what you like, what you don't like, what are your dreams, and more importantly to talk a little about our future. Our culture does not allow us to talk freely before engagement, but at least we can know a bit about each other before marriage. What do you say?"

'A sensible guy' Sandy thought, "Yes that is true, I am thankful, and I appreciate it. I was also wondering how to talk to you. But you go first," encouraged Sandy.

"That's good. I am happy you feel the same. Let me tell you about my parents. My mother and father have done a lot of hard work to get me where I am now. My father was neck deep in debts by the time I completed my education. They sacrificed everything for me. So I owe my life to them. If they had given up on me, I would have been toiling in the soil like my father as a common farmer; not that I think anything less of farmers, but that simply would have been too much for me. I started paying back the debts and thanks to you I can pay it back completely," Prakash said the last sentence with a kind of awkwardness.

Sandy was taken aback and thought, 'is it fair to put someone else in debt for the sake of paying back their own debts?' She looked at him silently, asking him to continue.

"Your silence tells me you understand my affection towards my parents. I just wanted to tell you I like you, and I will remember what you have done for our family, but I wanted to ask something else also. I do not want any misunderstandings in the future. After our marriage, I want my parents to come and live with us. I want to take care of them and give them everything they have forgone for me. I hope you understand?" asked Prakash imploringly.

"Yes I understand. I have no problem with it. Your parents are like my own parents. It would be our duty to look after them. I mean I would expect my brother to do the same for my parents. And I would do the same for my parents if necessary, I hope you understand that too," questioned Sandy closely.

"Yes sure, that would be of no problem," he seemed honest though hesitant. "So I have made myself clear to you. I guess you also have something to ask me. What is it? You can ask anything you want. Do not hesitate to talk. After marriage it would be very late," Prakash seemed relaxed by now.

Sandy was reluctant for a moment, but she had to ask, "As you know, I am in my final year of B.Com. I would like to do my masters, read further, and I am very much interested in working, that too, I hope for full-time. I wanted your opinion on that," Sandy's heart was beating fast. By the look on Prakash's face, she didn't know what he thought of it.

"Study? Job? Do your parents know how you felt about your studies? I mean I didn't know you had high aspirations," Prakash seemed perplexed.

"Yes they know, but they can only do so much. I hope you understand," Sandy closed her eyes for a moment and turned away to look at the roses and the butterflies in her garden, she thought how free the butterflies were. She was jealous of them.

"To speak the truth I have no issues regarding you pursuing further studies or doing a job, if you can manage a job and the house. A lot of women in city do that, but my parents are very conservative. They don't approve of women working. You know how it is," Prakash said in an upset voice, "And as my parents would be living with us, I do not think that would work out."

Thoughts flooded at once. Sandy understood his limitations, 'He is not the one for me. It would be a blunder to go ahead with this. I have to do what my heart says I am capable of. I am not capable of this. I am not some property or cattle, I marry a guy who is not ready to give his best to his wife, I put my parents in debts to pay the debts of my fiancé, this does not sound right. It is not fair, it is not fair to my parents, and I would not be able to live with the thought that my father and my brother would still be in debt, while she is 'happily' married.

Finally she spoke, "So tell me Prakash, you take dowry from my father, you take me away from my parents, you would not allow me to study or do a job, you expect me to be a good daughter to your parents, then what are you giving me? A mere gold chain of Mangalsutra? The honour of being your wife?"

By the time she realised she had spoken way out of her limit, it was too late. Prakash looked irritated, "So this is the real you then. I thought you were a sensible woman. If you wanted to read and do a job so much, why did you agree to marry then? You should have talked to your father instead of talking so rudely with me. I don't think we are getting married. I wanted a humble housewife. I do not want a rebellious girl as my wife, if you talk to me this way now, how would you talk to me and my parents when we are married?" and to Sandy's horror, he said, "The wedding is off. Thank God, this ended here, I would have been sorry all my life, if you had not spoken like this. A million thanks to you, my life would have been ruined." So saying, he left Sandy shaking in the garden, somehow the fragrance of the garden seemed to vanish and the roses looked pale.

As Prakash was leaving the house, Sandy's father came across him and froze when he saw the expression on Prakash's face. "Prakash, what happened son, you look angry?"

"Uncle, I cannot talk anything right now, my father will come and talk to you later. Sorry for leaving in a hurry." Sandy's father looked frightened and turned to look at Sandy for answers. Sandy knew the engagement was about to break. She has done the one thing she never intended to do; her parents would be ashamed of her now. She was scared, what had she done! She can live with her mistake, but her parents will not be able to take the shame. It will become hard for they will be ridiculed in the society.

She went to her father, made him sit on the sofa, sat beside him, and with care she started telling him what had happened. She hoped he would forgive her for what she had done. But there was a blank expression on his face, "Do you know what you have done stupid girl? Now you will never get married. How do you suppose we will live from now on? People talk, especially about the girl who broke her own engagement. I will go and talk to Prakash's father, may be he will forgive you and make Prakash understand that it was just your childish nature that you spoke that way."

As he was ready to go, Sandy stopped her father, "*Nanna* it was not my childish nature. I do not regret a word I said to him. I don't want you to go and apologise on my behalf. He is asking too much of what I can give him. If I give the family all they expect and if I do not follow my dreams, then I will be empty *Nanna*, your daughter will not survive such a life, I will be dead inside and just live for others."

Her father became angrier at this, "What ridiculous thoughts you have! What's all this? Dead inside, what does that mean? All the relatives and neighbours were right; too much of education to girls makes them lose logical sense."

"*Nanna*, please try to understand, I have my destiny to fulfill..."

"Shut up! Enough is enough. You have left us nowhere. We had a dignified life here, living calmly, now you have ruined everything," her father raised his hand to slap her when her mother interrupted him, "What are you doing? You should not be shouting at a girl like that. Control yourself." Sandy never saw her father like this. He turned red with anger, but as her mother tried to calm him down, he became quiet and after a few minutes, which seemed like eternity, he began speaking in a grave tone, "Just tell me you will agree to marry, it's not too late." Sandy looked into her father's eyes, there was hurt and a sense of betrayal in his eyes, but she knew she could not marry that person, "With all respect *Nanna*, I cannot marry Prakash. Please understan..."

"Stop it. I do not understand you. May be I can never understand you. But you have disobeyed me. Even after giving a chance you have refused to obey me. You are dead for me forever!"

"What! *Nanna* just try to hear me. . . ," Sandy was horrified. Tears trickled down her cheeks.

"Never try to talk to me again. This is my final decision. Though you have no respect for me, I have respect for Prakash's father, I will go and apologise to him. You have given me a nice payback for loving you."

Sandy saw her father leave. She saw him go through the main door through her blurred eyes filled with water. She fell down on the floor in a heap. Her only thought was, 'What have I done? Why does he not understand that it is not my fault? Have I lost my *Nanna* forever?' The thought crushed her inside and she started weeping on the floor when her mother caught her, "Don't cry my child, don't cry, everything is supposed to be for our own good, do not lose hope. Your father said those words in anger. He did not mean it. In some days, everything will be fine. Just go and tell him that you will obey him and are willing to get married. Everything will be fine," Sandy's mother patted her back and ran her hand over her head.

"Haven't you heard anything that I have said? Don't you see any sense in what I have said?" filled with tears in her eyes Sandy asked her mother.

"Don't be foolish Sandhya. This is your fate, accept it!" even her mother was angered.

"May be it's for my own good that this marriage is not taking place *Amma*, have you ever thought of that?" Sandy questioned her mother closely.

"When did you become so foolishly stubborn? Don't be so selfish; think about your family too."

EVEN AFTER MORE than a year, she remembered the incident very clearly. Sandy smiled at what her mother had said. In real sense, she was thinking about her family, but they thought she was selfish. The events that followed were scary, but she had to do what she believed in. Her brother and she had a big fight over it. After the fight, things were not the same. All the relatives were gone, but not before insulting her. Her father never talked to her for the next two months, her mother would talk to her in a very angry manner. Her brother became totally aloof from her. She became a stranger in her own house. She could not take it anymore.

One day she packed her bags, took some money she had with her and said bye to everyone in the family. She planned to go to the city and find a job for herself. She had to do what she believed she wanted to do. She found a girls hostel and talked to the warden on the phone, she seemed a nice lady, the hostel fee was also reasonable. She gave the address of the hostel to her mother who was sure she would fail and come away from the city. That was the hardest part of her life. When your own family is not your family anymore, nothing else seems to be a big problem. She got a job in a bank call centre in just two months and from then, she had never turned back to regret. In just a few months,

Sneha joined her and things have never been better. May be in these few months, Sneha might have written to her, so she could not get the letters she had written. She was angry that her mother did not forward the letters to her even though she had the address. But thinking of what Sneha had gone through made her problems look much smaller. 'Your own child killed by your husband and in-laws is hideous, the biggest betrayal of all'. Though she had regretted the decision she had taken for a few months, now the decision seems to be the best decision she has ever made.

'Now I am not jealous of the butterflies anymore.'

IT'S BEEN A few months since the news flash and Sneha's moment of truth with Sandy. Everything seemed to have become normal. When Sneha knew of what Sandy had been through, her respect for Sandy increased, for her courage, her love of the family, and her clear thought of what life should be like, and how she dealt her life after the incident. She could have given up easily, but she did not. Sneha's new beginning also was not so smooth either. When on that fateful night, she boarded the bus she did not have a good education or a promise of a future. All she thought was to get out of the prison. She called up at Sandy's house. Sandy's mother was on the phone.

"Good morning aunty, is Sandy home?"

"Arey is this Sneha, how are you, how are your in-laws, I heard you were pregnant, which month is it?"

"Oh! I am fine aunty," she hesitated for a while, "I lost my baby aunty."

"What! I don't know what to say Sneha."

When she asked if she could talk to Sandy, her mother said that she no longer lived with them and that she was living in the city. Though it seemed strange, she was in no mood to question the reason. She just asked Sandy's address in the city. When she got it, she came to the city and she stood at the door, trembling. Her hopes that Sandy would help came true. Sandy was really the best friend anyone could get. They both thought for a while on what Sneha can do to earn a living. Then suddenly, Sandy remembered that she designed and did good embroidery for saris and *ghagras*. They tried many big workshops, where such work was going on, but it was not that easy. So for sometime before she could work in a big workshop, Sneha started doing embroidery for the neighbourhood houses; she earned a good amount of money. Then one day a Marwadi neighbour, Mrs. Sehgal, for whom Sneha had done some silver *Jardosi* work on a white sari, came to her excited.

"Sneha, yesterday I went to the marriage of one of my relatives, there I met a lady Mrs. Ayyangar. She knew that I did not buy this sari in any of the shops just by looking at it. She looked at the work you have done and loved the work. She wanted to meet you. I told her your address, she said she would come and meet you at your house at one o'clock. She must be coming here at anytime now. I felt it would do a lot of good. Good hardworking people like you are meant to prosper and I think this will be a chance for you to improve your business," Mrs. Sehgal's eyes twinkled.

"Thank you Mrs. Sehgal. But my own business? I did not understand. She might be coming here to get a sari worked on, why would I have my own business?" puzzled Sneha.

"Arey, I totally forgot to mention. She is the owner of half a dozen boutiques. She has a design team of her own and her boutiques are known for their individualistic creations." Mrs. Sehgal seemed very excited.

"Boutique owner? Wow! That would be great! Now I get it, why you are so excited. Thank you Mrs. Sehgal, thank you very much."

"No problem dear. It's your talent that will take you places."

"Thank you Mrs. Sehgal for having so much confidence in me. What is her name?"

“She is Mrs. Priyadarshini Ayyangar. Her husband is a CEO of a software company. They were not born rich, but they worked their way up in life and often help people with real talent. My friends told me all about her. Oh! Hundred years for Mrs. Ayyangar. Here she comes!”

A Corolla came in front of the modest house of Sneha and Sandy. The car looked out of place in that street. But when Mrs. Ayyangar got out of the car, she did not look out of place. Sneha thought she was an idol of simplicity. If she did not get down the car, no one would have guessed that she was the owner of so many boutiques.

“Good afternoon Mrs. Sehgal. I guess this is Sneha. Good afternoon Sneha.” She shook hands with both of the ladies there.

“Good afternoon Mrs. Ayyangar. I am glad to meet you.”

“Oh! Please no formalities. Call me Priya. I am also very glad to meet you.”

Sneha thought ‘No formalities?’ But her personality demanded respect in a subtle way. How can she not be formal?

“I saw your work on the sari Mrs. Sehgal was wearing yesterday. I thought it was unique and I just wanted to meet you straight away. There is originality in your designs, I guess mostly influenced by villages and its distinct arts.” Mrs. Ayyangar questioned.

“Yes Priya madam, I come from a village and most of the things that I have seen in the village had influenced my work. I am glad you liked it.”

“You can just call me Priya. Can you show me some of your work?”

“Oh! Sorry madam, I did not even ask you to come in, please do come in, be seated, I will bring my work.”

As Mrs. Ayyangar sat in the drawing room, she looked around the house; she liked it that this girl was hard working and neat.

The girls these days, 'uff' she thought, they don't even clean their rooms; they depend on their mothers for everything. She liked her hospitality. She had tea and looked at her designs and some saris she had worked on and still had not delivered. Overall, she was very much impressed. "Sneha, I am very impressed with your work. I would like a fresh approach of yours in my boutiques, not influenced by western style, pure Indian. We will start a new collection. I would like you to be working with a team in developing the work you are doing, but your work is rough in some areas, you can work on that to improve."

"That would be great madam, thank you for giving me this opportunity."

"What are your educational qualifications Sneha?"

"I am afraid I did not read much. I completed my 10+2." She felt nervous telling this, lest the lady might change her opinion.

"Oh! That's a shame, but that is not a problem, you can resume your studies doing this job. You know dear, if you have better educational qualifications, I can give you a better job position than what I am offering you right now. So can you work harder and do both reading and working at the same time?"

Sneha's eyes were filled with tears, "Thank you madam, thank you very much. I do not know what to say. Yes I will surely do my best in both the areas."

And that's how she landed in a dream job and continued her education. She did not have time to think of the wrong done to her baby or her past life until the day when she saw the news on television. It brought back memories and the pain she had gone through.

A few months passed by after the incident and she regained her strength back. She was earning good money. She was saving it, not spending too much of it other than for the needs she had. She was quite content with her life.

One day early in the morning, while both Sandy and Sneha were getting ready for the day, there was a sharp tap on the door.

"Pearl, can you look who has come?"

"Ok."

When Sneha opened the door, she was stunned to see the person standing in front of her. She could not believe her eyes, it was her husband. Satish looked tired and somehow this tiredness made his features more cruel.

"How are you Sneha? Can I come in?" He did not wait for her to speak; he came into the room and sat in the chair. "You have a good house here." Sneha was still dazed to speak anything. She could not believe what was happening. Thoughts ran in her mind, 'How did he know I was here, of course Sandy's mother knew the address.'

Sandy came out of the bedroom, "Who is it Pearl?" and she too stood there dumbstruck seeing Satish. "You bas* what are you doing in our house. Get lost! Get out of here, who asked you to come in?" Sandy burst out.

"I came here to visit my wife, Sneha you are still my wife, aren't you? Or do you have a boyfriend now or what?" asked Satish very sarcastically.

Sneha was just looking in the direction of Sandy, and then she caught the look of Satish, she wanted to know if he had any guilt at all. "It's okay Sandy, let me deal with him. I think I should talk to him and better get over with it. You leave for the office. I will be okay."

Sandy looked surprised, "But. . . ."

"I will be okay Sandy, I need to talk to him," said Sneha sternly.

"If you want to talk to him, it's okay with me, but I am not leaving you alone with that criminal," Sandy said scornfully.

"Who are you calling criminal? Mind your own business madam. Do not poke your nose in others' affairs," Satish spoke sharp.

“The cat closes its eyes, drinks the milk, and thinks no one knows what it had done. Pearl if you want to talk to him, you can, but I will be in the bedroom. Just call me if you need me.” She shot another glance at Satish and went away.

When Sandy left, Sneha turned to Satish, she had gained her strength, “Why did you come here?”

“Why does a husband come to his wife? Because you are my wife and you are supposed to be with me. I forgive you that you ran away like that. It took a lot of time to know where you were. You never told me about your best friend. She calls you Pearl, aye. Nice.”

“What about your fatherly duties then, Satish? Did you ever think of that? I know what you did and you are a fool if you think I am coming back with you.”

“Past is past. It has been nearly a year. Can’t you forget the past and come back?”

“I will come back with you, but on one condition. Give me back my ‘Chitti’ and I will come with you this instant.” Sneha was breathing fast, trying to control her rage.

“Do not talk rubbish. You know I cannot do that. I did a mistake, can’t you just forgive me and can’t we just go on with our lives?” Satish looked away.

“You killed my daughter. You are a killer!” shouted Sneha. Hearing this, Satish jumped up angry, was about to say something, but then Sandy came out, “Pearl are you alright?” she saw tears in Sneha’s eyes and turned to Satish, “I think you better go.”

Satish wanted to say something, but seeing how serious Sandy was, he said he would come back at some other time and went away.

“What did that bas* want from you?” asked Sandy.

“He wanted me to go home with him,” Sneha now controlled herself.

"What! After all that he expects you to forget everything and go away with him!"

"Pretty much that's the situation. He says it so coldly, 'I did a mistake'. He must have some kind of guilt Sandy, how can a person kill someone and be without guilt? She was his daughter too."

"Do not upset yourself by thinking what he felt or did not feel. The only thing you can do is to do the right thing. Let's go to work, don't even think of staying back and thinking about what had happened. Work will clear your mind. Now get ready, you are getting late."

"Yes, you are right." Sneha hurried to get ready.

Though her work kept her busy, there was one thing going on in her mind. What was she to do now? There was no way she was getting back with him. But she wanted to punish him; looking at him made her hate him much more. Her hatred for him made her stronger. She wanted to prosecute him. But she had no evidence. What was she to do? She had to contact a lawyer. Then at last, she decided it was time to start a life without the shadow of her husband over her. She decided that would be the best thing. She wanted to talk to Sandy about this, but she was sure that Sandy would say she had taken the right decision. She was excited to talk to Sandy that evening. She knew she could count on Sandy for helping her out through this decision.

SANDY LOVED THE job she was doing. The American Bank was a great place to work. Her good communication skills and her humour were her best qualifications, she found out later. Her degree was only nominal; thousands of people in the state have the degree. She prepared for all the five rounds of tests and interview along with her hostel friend. She passed through all the rounds with flying colors and landed in this job. She never thought she would work in such a great office with the starting salary that would pay her rent and make her independent. She thanked God every time she saw her office. Sure sometimes the work was a burden and would make her stay over time till late in the night, but it was worth every minute of it.

That particular day, while talking to the HR manager, she got a call on her cell phone. When she saw the number displayed on her cell screen, she did not know what to expect. It was her home number, why would her parents call her after such a long time. They stopped talking to her since her engagement broke up and since she came away, even her mother has stopped talking to her. There must be something really wrong, her pulse sounded quick, she hesitated to lift the phone, but praying to God, she finally pressed the answering button, "Hello?"

"Hello Sandhya?" Her mother sounded very tensed.

"*Amma*! What happened? Something wrong?" She could not help wonder, it has been ages since she called her mother *Amma*.

"Sandhya, come home as soon as possible, your brother had a terrible accident. Your father is not able to hold himself, he does not say anything about you, but he misses you terribly. Your brother is in the Government Hospital right now, come soon. You will come home, won't you?"

"What! Is he fine? What are the doctors saying?" Sandy tensed up.

When Sandy asked that question, her mother started crying, "Your brother is in a coma, he has been like that since morning, I wanted you to be here, your father and I need your support, come home quick."

"COMA! Oh my God! I will be there by evening *Amma*. I am starting just now, don't worry *Amma*, everything will be fine." Sandy disconnected the call. 'Will everything be alright?' the thought sent a shiver through her body.

Sandy called up Sneha and told her what had happened. Sneha thought for a little while, Sandy needed her, but she had to face her parents. Sandy sensed her problem, "Pearl, do not worry. I just wanted to inform you. You need not come with me, just take care of yourself."

Sneha heard the shaky voice of Sandy and decided instantly, "No Sandy, I have no problem coming with you. I will be there for you whenever you need me. Come home, we will meet there and start off immediately." Sandy felt strong again, "I have such a good friend. See you at home." Both took leave, reached home, packed some clothes, drew some money out from the ATM, and sat in the bus to 'home'. They did not know what lay ahead of them, but one thing common between both the friends was that their village has become a memory, a strange place that belonged to the past. Both prayed that their beloved brother would get out of the coma safe and sound.

The bus gave a sudden jerk and started, leaving a huge cloud of smoke into the passersby's faces. It seemed as if the smoke has enveloped Sandy's mind, nothing seemed clear, she was suddenly scared at the thought of her brother not being able to make it, just then Sneha took her hand and pressed it in an assuring way. Sandy turned towards Sneha and looked into her eyes. There was kindness and strength in her eyes. The sparkle in her eyes cleared the smoke in her heart. There seemed no need for words; just a reassuring glance is all a person needs to get on in life. The village was about five hours away from the city and both adjusted their seats comfortably for the five-hour bumpy road ahead.

As Sandy looked out of the window, waking up from the doziness, she saw the similar contour of the land, somehow that never changes, the way rocks are laid and the way trees grow. She always thought that every town or village has an individual setting of its own, even with everyday changes, the place remains the same in its heart. The same banyan trees ran past their bus, where she used to hang on the branches all day long in the long afternoons. The colourful ice-cream carts being pushed by not-so-cheerful man. The bus stopped at the bus station. A flood of people rushed out, no one would stop even for a second. Sandy and Sneha got down the bus; they could think of nothing than rushing to the hospital as soon as possible. They got into a rickshaw and started off for the hospital. When they reached near to the hospital, they saw Sandy's mother out near the counter of medicines and ran towards her.

"*Amma*!" She ran to her mother and hugged her. Though she was tensed, she felt relieved as soon as she hugged her mother. She felt whole again. Her mother started crying looking at her, Sandy felt her mother sigh with relief. She felt good after a long time. "How is Rakesh, *Amma*? What did the doctors say?" Sandy saw her mother's eyes were sadder than she had ever seen, she thought, 'She missed me!'

"Oh thank God! Your brother is out from coma. The doctors say that some blood had accumulated in his brain, but after sometime it got cleared. Just after I talked to you, I came back to the room where he was kept and then he woke up, about an hour or so. He is sleeping now, he lost some blood."

"Oh that's great. Sneha and I were both very tensed about what might be the situation."

"Sneha! It's been a long time since I have heard from her. Her parents said she went away to the city leaving her husband." Sandy's mother looked at Sneha, she smiled back. "She is a good girl, there must be a strong reason why she did that. I guess she is with you. I thought so. You girls were inseparable since you were kids." And she smiled.

Sandy saw her mother smile and she thought it was the most beautiful smile in the world. She hugged her mother lest it would be the last time.

"Don't worry Sandhya, everything will be fine." She lifted Sandhya up and turned to Sneha, "Sneha! Why are you standing so far? Come here." Sneha came near her and Sandy's mother hugged her, "Thank you Sneha for talking care of her, my child.

I will always be thankful to you." Sneha's heart jumped with joy.

"Tell me *Amma*, how is *Nanna* doing. Is he still angry at me?"

"If you want to know how your father is, go and ask him. He is with your brother in the room. Come with me, I will show you the room."

As they were led by Sandy's mother, they saw troubled faces in different inpatient rooms, some hopeful, some not so very hopeful. Sandy's heart skipped a beat with joy when she saw her father looking up from the chair by the side of her brother's bandaged body. By the look in her father's eye, she knew that her father was expecting her.

"You came at last Sandy? So it had to be the reason of your brother's accident that had to make you come to 'your' home?"

"I thought you were all angry with me *Nanna*. No one was talking to me. What was I supposed to do? I thought you felt I was a burden to you father. I could not stay here and wait for things to get better. I wanted to do something. So I went away. I always thought of coming back, but I didn't know how you all would react. But I always thought of you *Nanna*."

After a moment of silence, which seemed a decade to Sandy, her father said, "I am glad you came here Sandhya. Your mother needs you (which meant her father needed her). Your brother is doing fine now. He will be alright in a week, it seems. He will not wake up before sometime, go home and get fresh." He patted her head and smiled.

Sandy now at last felt her life was complete. There was a big empty space in her heart all these days, now she had no complaints with life. Everything was perfect. She went to her brother's side and looked at him. His face was full of bandages. She could see his long eyelashes and remembered the times she used to tease him that he was a girl because he had such long thick lashes. He was breathing normally as if he was in deep sleep. Her naughty brother, who teased her by pulling ribbon from her hair, was going to be alright. Sandy felt peaceful after a long time.

Both Sneha and Sandy went back to Sandy's home. It was a village and it took no time for Sneha's parents to know that she was here too. Sneha dreaded to be confronted by her parents. She knew they would not understand her. Her parents were orthodox and no matter what, according to them, a married woman's place was always with the husband. She believed in that too, but that was a long time ago.

Sandy understood what Sneha was thinking about, "Pearl, don't worry. You know I will be by your side, even when your parents come to talk to you. But for now get ready, we will start off in half an hour to the hospital."

"I will be ready in five minutes," hurried Sneha.

Just when they were about to leave for the hospital, both saw Sneha's mother coming their way. Seeing her mother brought back warmth in Sneha's heart. She hurried towards her mother. "How are you *Amma*?"

"We were fine, but thanks to you now our lives have become hell. What is the meaning of all this? Have you become crazy? You leave your husband and go to the city, and look at your shamelessness; you came back to this place and live with at your friend's place. You don't want us to live in peace. First you runaway from your in-laws leaving us at the mercy of their scorn and then you come back, we will not be able to walk in this place with a million questions arising from each vulgar mouth."

Sneha knew exactly these words would come from her mother's mouth. But for a second, she felt that her mother might have missed her. "*Amma*, I missed you, didn't you miss me?"

"What kind of a silly question is that? Of course we missed you. But there are a lot of things to be considered. We need to get on with the standards of the society, not become a matter of ridicule instead. And you have done that exactly. Now we are suffering because of you. Don't expect my forgiveness for what you have done. I have called your husband, informing that you have come here. So now don't think of running away again." warned her mother and went away steaming and leaving Sneha thirsty for a hug.

Sandy put her hand on Sneha's shoulder, "Pearl, don't be sad, their whole life has revolved around orthodox thoughts and deeds, don't expect them to change, at least not in this short time. But till that time, I am your family. You know that."

Sneha settled herself, "Yes, I know you are my family. Let's go and see big brother."

When Sandy arrived at the hospital room, her brother was awake and waiting for her. "I guess father told you that I have come to see you?"

"No Sandy, I knew you would come here, you would not be able to leave your brother alone, not when I am in this situation." Seeing her brother smiling with his lip swollen, was definitely going to be one of her most memorable moments of her life. She was going to tease him in the future, she smiled in herself, but for now she was relieved that her brother has regained consciousness. She sat by his side, they held their hands, and they spoke all the words they wanted to speak to each other. They had unspoken feelings of one year to share.

Having made their peace (or at least so) with their families, both returned to their lives.

IT HAD BEEN a few months since the accident, Sandy's union with her family, and Sneha's peace with her family. One day out of nowhere, Sneha got a letter from her parents. The letter said that they were coming to stay with her for some time and wanted to talk to her about something important (which only meant that they wanted her to go back to her in-laws' family). They came two days after the letter arrived. Sneha tried to prepare for the interrogation and negotiation of the family.

Though she expected her parents, she did not expect her husband to come along with them. Sneha absolutely refused to speak to him after the day he came to their house. She felt very strongly about giving him a divorce and getting on with her life, for better or for worse. Most of the talking was done by her mother, "Satish told us what had happened. I can imagine now why you must have reacted in such a silly way. But past is past, nothing can be done about it. Whatever problems you face, you have to work over it and I think you should return back to him. And he is very sorry for what he had done. He deeply regrets it Sneha. Just listen to him."

This shook Sneha, "He is sorry for what he has done. Mother, don't you know what is the punishment for killers in our country? They hang them till death. It is not a petty thing that I should forgive him. And he did not ask me for forgiveness nor did I feel he is sorry for what he had done."

"Sneha, such rudeness, in front of your parents! Have I taught you anything at all? You sometimes make me doubt if you were my daughter." Sneha's mother saw shock in her eyes and calmed down, "Try to understand me Sneha, he says he is sorry for what he has done. Just listen to what he has to say."

Sneha turned towards Satish, "What do you want to say to me? Why have you come here? Haven't I told you that I didn't want to be your wife again?"

"I am sorry for what I have done Sneha. I am saying it sincerely. I was under a lot of pressure. I knew I could not earn a good amount of money to save for dowry. That would mean a lot of debts. Even for Sweety, we are facing a lot of debt to get her married. This debt itself could take us a lot of time to recover from. How can I take another debt and dream of paying it back? If after our first baby girl, what if we could not have any baby boys, then it would have become impossible for us to do anything.

Mother was also saying the same, so I did what I thought was the best thing to do. I am sorry. But I want you to come back. Moreover, Sweety's marriage has been arranged. It is a nice match. Her marriage will be in a month or two. But...... the thing is they heard some rumours about you and they wanted to make sure that these rumours were not true. We told them you were recuperating from illness, after the death of your baby, in your mother's house. Now you like Sweety too, wouldn't you do something for her to get settled in her life nicely?"

"So the apologies, the act of reforming, were all for your sister's marriage?" Sneha eyes reddened.

"No, no, I just wanted you to know that it will be Sweety's marriage and you could help out."

"Okay, I will come to Sweety's marriage," started Sneha calmly, "But there is one condition."

"What is it?"

With a coldness so alien to Sneha, she said, "Give me my daughter!"

"Don't be absurd!" turned away Satish with a feeling of disgust and anger.

"Did you tell Sweety's in-laws about how you KILLED my daughter?" shouted Sneha hysterically. "DON'T YOU EVER COME BACK AGAIN. I WILL NEVER EVER COME BACK TO YOU. This is my final decision and I will send you the divorce papers and if possible, I will file a case against you and send you to prison. Even if I lose, I will file the case till my last breath. This is a promise Satish and unlike you, I keep my promises." Her mother was about to say something, "Mother, I have given enough respect to you all along, but not this time. Just go away. I will talk to you later."

Sneha decided that whatever may be the future, she would file a case against Satish and fight him to make sure he would not hurt another baby and make it a lesson for everyone who intends to kill baby girls.

✧

SANDY ALSO HAD to face a ghost of the past. One weekend, Sandy went to see her family, and her brother recouped very fast. Sandy felt truly happy that everything was going so well. She was working with more enthusiasm at the office and was due for a promotion. She got back into her family and it seemed there was no limit to what she could do. She was inspired by Sneha's courage, her confidence. If every woman was as strong as she was, then there would be no gender bias and no more illegal abortions or killing of the girls. Sneha had turned into a solid role model for her, going strong every day. She was with her mother in the kitchen tasting the hot dishes she had prepared, when her father called her. She ran from the kitchen to the drawing room.

"Yes *Nanna*, what is it?"

"Sandhya I wanted to talk something important, come and sit down by my side," her father patted on the sofa. She sat by his side and looked at her father questioningly. "What happened in the past is past, so I have found another match for you." Seeing the reaction in Sandy's face, "Oh don't worry, I have talked to them. The boy is a lecturer in a college in the city, his name is Sanjeev Prasad. They know that you work and that you have ambitions of reading further. They were looking for a bride exactly like you. I am getting old Sandy, I want to get you married and my duty for you will be fulfilled. What do you say?"

"I don't know what to think father. I haven't thought about marriage, yes sometimes I feel that it may be late after sometime, but father right now I am thinking about my career."

"Yes I understand. I respect that. You have your own feelings and ambitions. But when you are with a life partner who understands what you want to do and supports you, you can manage all these even after marriage. Try and understand my child. I just want you to be happy."

Sandy saw an anxious look in her father's tired eyes. She thought, 'they have faced so many problems because of me, if only I could give them some peace.' "Ok father, I am okay with your decision, but I want to talk to the guy before I take my decision father. Is that ok?"

"Yes I thought that was appropriate. Even the boy wants to talk to you before we fix anything. It is all good Sandy, it is all good. I have a good feeling about this." There was a look of relief on her father's face.

"Father, I just wanted to ask you one more thing. How much dowry do they expect?"

"Don't get concerned about all that again, it was all considered between us elders and I am happy with the dowry they are asking," he left smiling.

Sandy was not satisfied with the answer. She went straight up to her mother, "Mother, did you know about the match? How much dowry are they expecting?"

Hearing Sandy's tone, her mother said in a serious tone, "Sandy, we have forgiven what you have done, but that does not mean you can do all you want to do. We are your parents and intend to do only what is best for you. Anyway it is better to be clear with you. I do not want any confusion. They expect a dowry of 3 lakhs. It is reasonable for a lecturer to ask so much."

"THREE LAKHS! You cannot afford that much. I know that you have saved only 1.5 lakhs. I guess the rest you are going to take a debt. And Rakesh has to deal with it all."

"Don't be so dramatic Sandy. You know that is a reasonable dowry. Anyway, your brother need not deal with it. He would also get a dowry when he is married and that can cover all the costs, even your marriage costs. We have already seen a good match for your brother."

Sandy's head was reeling. She was stuck in a vicious cycle. The reason she was giving a dowry was to get settled with a financially stable person, but her parents were stuck in a debt beyond their reach. And then to pay their debt, they take dowry from another girl, who may not be able to afford such a dowry. And this cycle goes on and on. She decided what she had to do.

A day was fixed when Sandy was to meet Prasad.

"Hi, I am Prasad."

"Good morning, I am Sandhya, my friends call me Sandy."

"I am a commerce lecturer in a private college. I like my job. I know you work as a sales executive in American Bank. That is a cool job."

"Thanks."

"I like travelling, reading books, and movies. I train my students for dramas also. I enjoy being with my students. What are your hobbies?"

"That is good; one should always love what they do. I do not have much of hobbies. I was always good at reading. I like crossword puzzles, chess, and doing quizzes."

"Oh that's good. What are the qualities you expect in your future husband?"

"To be honest, I didn't think much of it. I guess I just wanted some freedom to take my own decisions regarding my life, like choosing to go to work or study more. That is actually too much to ask for a girl in this village."

"Yes I understand. This is not a problem only in the villages, it is there in the city too. Some of my students, girls who are highly intellectual, have to sometimes abide by their parent's rules and leave their studies in the middle, only few girls have the guts to do what they really want to do. And I understand you are one of those girls who want to do what is right."

This surprised Sandy, "Yes I am. Prasad I like you, but I want to ask you something."

"Thank you, I like you too. I am an honest guy, and you can ask me anything."

"Will you marry me without the dowry?"

This took Prasad by surprise, "Without dowry!"

Sandy seemed disheartened by the reaction, "Yes."

"Oh! I thought your parents were okay with it."

"Yes, my parents are okay with it, but I know they cannot afford it. And frankly I am against dowry. I can only say this. So please say that you did not like me, to your parents. I hope you understand. If my parents would know that I told you my opinion regarding dowry to you, I will lose my parents. I don't want that to happen. But I cannot lose my beliefs too. I have honour and self-respect that I am not willing to let go off."

Prasad looked a little taken aback, but then he realised what was going on, "I respect that. Ok then, bye."

"Bye," Sandy took a deep breath.

Prasad turned back, "I wish all the best for your future. I am glad I met you." He smiled and went away.

Sandy did not understand whether he meant it in a good way or bad way. But overall she was happy that she handled the situation very nicely. The next day, she came back to the city and told what had happened to Sneha. How she faced the same problem all over again and how she handled the situation.

In the upcoming days, Sandy's parents called her up saying there was no call from Prasad's parents. Sandy's mother grew suspicious and asked Sandy if she had anything to do with this. Sandy said 'no' without hesitation. Sandy knew that after waiting for some time, her parents would again look for a match for her. But now she knew exactly what she had to do.

✧

IT WAS NEARLY two years since both of them had been living together. Both were going strong in their careers and more confident each day. Sneha one day woke up early in the morning and woke Sandy up.

"What will happen to me if you get married and go away? I will be all alone Sandy. I am scared."

"Whaaaat aaaare youuuu saaaaying? . . . . I want to sleep some more. AAAhh...You also sleep for some more time. I am not going anywhere," yawned Sandy.

"No Sandy I am really scared. I have become estranged from my parents. I may not be able to get married. I lost a daughter. And you will also get married some day. What then? What will I do?"

Sandy rubbed her eyes and sat up, "even though I get married, I will just rent a place nearby and we will take care of each other."

"But that is not enough, is it Sandy? I mean, I want a family."

"Cool down Pearl. What happened to you? Why are you all tensed up? Have you found anyone special or what?" Sandy poked her finger to tickle Sneha.

"Very funny, don't tease me. I am serious."

"Then?"

"As I have been earning well, I will adopt a child after saving some good amount of money in the bank. What do you say? I am really excited about this idea."

"Adopt a child! That sounds a bit extreme Sneha."

"I have thought all sides of it Sandy. I have thought it out every way practicably possible. I am sure this is a great way to help someone out and in the process help myself too. I miss my little girl Sandy. If I adopt a girl, then I can see my daughter in that child."

"I understand you Sneha. I think it is a great idea. I know you will be a great mother for that little girl."

"But I have one little detail to ask you. It finally depends on what you would answer me."

"Depends on me?"

"Yes, you see I know my parents will not support me on this. Frankly speaking, I am dead to them. I don't know if I will get married or not. The only family I have is you Sandy. So I want you to be the godmother of the child I adopt. It means if something happens to me then you will have to take care of the child. You will be her guardian. So I want you to think about it and answer me. No hurry. Take your time."

"Oh! That is a big decision Sneha. A very noble thought of yours, but I do not know if I can do it or not."

"I know this is a big decision. But what would you do if I had my own daughter and something happened to me and there is no one to take care of my daughter? Just think in those terms and answer that question honestly. Then you will know your answer." Sneha smiled. Sandy never saw Pearl so confident. And she had no signs of past in her. She was whole again. The thought of having a daughter cleared the pain and made her the girl she knew at a younger age. The whole day Sneha seemed happy. She knew Sneha was already dreaming of a child now. She thought it over, 'what if there was no one to take care of my child in the future, wouldn't I expect the same from her' and it makes perfect sense that Pearl would take care of her daughter than anyone else.

The next day Sandy went to Sneha, "I heartily agree to become your daughter's godmother, but there is one condition."

Sneha was excited, "I will agree to any condition."

"The condition is that you will also become the godmother of my child in the future."

"Oh yes, I would, I would. Ohhhh! Thank you Sandy. You are the best. I will apply for adoption today itself." Sneha kissed Sandy and ran away.

Sandy thought Sneha must have grown wings, just thinking of a child of her own.

⟡

THE NEXT DAY, Sandy got a call from her mother. She sounded excited on the phone. She asked Sandy to come home immediately. Even when Sandy asked what was it that her mother was so eager about, "You remember Sanjeev Prasad, don't you?"

"Prasad! Yes, he is the one who came to see me a few months ago, probably three or four months ago. What does he want? They did not respond for so long." Sandy was confused why he came into the picture again.

"Yes Sandy, his parents have called your father again this morning. They are coming to talk to us this weekend. I think this match will be final. You are going to get married. I mean this is the only reason they have contacted us after so many months. Come soon this weekend." Sandy thought this was something she did not expect at all. Her mother was right, why else would they contact their parents after such a long time. She said bye to her mother and told Sneha what had happened. Sneha was sure that this meant really good news. She was praying to God that everything turn favourable.

When Sandy went home, her father smiled at her in a mysterious way. He just said, "You are lucky."

She did not understand why he said so. As she went in to greet her mother, she hurried her, "Get fresh, Prasad is coming here to talk to you."

"Prasad is coming? What is going on *Amma*?"

"You will know in a few hours, now get fresh. And you are one lucky girl." The same curious smile passed over her mother's lips.

Finally when Prasad arrived and they sat together to talk, Sandy asked him what was going on.

"It has been a long time since I talked to you. I liked the way you talked that day, you were honest and knew what you wanted out of your life. I knew you were the girl for me, but the decision was not just mine alone. I had to take the permission of my father and mother too. So I went back to my parents and explained to them that I was against dowry and that I wanted to marry you without the dowry. But of course you know that there is this image in the society that the more the dowry, the more worthy your son is. They wouldn't listen to me. They thought of finding some other good match for me, but I was persistent in what I had to say. A girl with honour and self-respect is the best partner I can find than any other girl. They tried for all these months, but finally gave up. So now I stand before you, asking you to marry me."

Sandy did not know what to say. She felt that this was not true. She felt it was a dream. The thought of marriage was in the distant future for her. So that's why her father and mother were so mysterious today. She liked the way Prasad reacted. He did not give any false hopes to her or her parents, went home, did all the work that was necessary and came back with a perfect solution. He was a man of word and honour. She knew he was the one for her. She said, "Yes."

The marriage date was fixed one month after that day and no one really had enough time to take care of the preparations. She went back to Sneha, told her what had happened. Sneha's eyes filled with tears of joy, "We will be friends forever." Sandy thought, after her marriage, she would look for a suitable man for Sneha, 'she deserves to be happy'. She took a leave for a month and returned to her home. Sneha promised her she would design a beautiful, unique wedding sari for her friend. Everything was running smoothly. Sneha sent her 'the sari'. It was the most exquisite sari Sandy had ever seen. The red silk sari, with a combination of simple embroidery and *Jardosi* work of golden beads and tiny golden springs, looked exquisite. Sneha was supposed to come three days before the marriage, but Sneha had some work, it was marriage season and big marriages needed special attention from her. She promised that she will be there at the time of Sandy's wedding.

It was the day of the marriage. The sky looked promising. All the songs from movies with the celebrations of marriage were being played by the music band. The red and blue striped tents now stood in the open place around Sandy's house and people were hurrying in and out of the house. There was an echo of laughter everywhere one went. The children played hide and seek in the tents, hiding behinds the chairs that were arranged for the guests to sit. Sandy now and then came out of the room and looked out of the window for any signs of Sneha coming. She knew she would come straight to her, but she couldn't just sit and wait for her. She tried calling her up at her cell, but it was switched off. There were only few hours left for the big event in her life, but her best friend was still not here. Sandy thought 'she must be on her way home, may be that's why her cell was switched off, there was no signal or some other problem. Something didn't seem right. She would have called me before she got into the bus.'

It was just a few minutes before marriage, still Sneha was no where to be seen. Her cell phone was not responding either. Sandy took a deep breath. She had no choice, but to marry without her Pearl by her side. With all the rituals of a classic Indian marriage, Sandhya was married to Sanjeev Prasad. Sandy was very worried by now. Pearl would not have missed the marriage, whatever be the situation. Elders were coming and giving blessings to the newly weds when Sandy saw her cell phone ring, she saw Pearl flash on the screen, she tried to see Pearl in the crowd, but she did not see her, she lifted the phone, "Hello. Pearl, where are you? I cannot believe you missed my marriage, I will kill you for this!"

"Hello is this Sandy? I am nurse Pragnya speaking here."

"Nurse Pragnya? Yes I am Sandy. This is my friend's phone, her name is Sneha, has she lost the phone?"

"No madam, she has not lost her phone. I got your friend's name from the office ID she was wearing. She is in the hospital.

She has fallen down from the steps of her office building and she struck her head to a concrete blocker and was fatally wounded. She has lost a lot of blood. She is in the ICU ward. Her cell had the most recent number of yours and so I called you up. Can you inform her family? She is in St. Maria's Hospital at Mahatma Gandhi Road. Please make some financial arrangements too madam. When can I expect you?"

"Five hours!" That was all she could manage to speak. She caught Prasad's hand, "We need to rush to the city, please take me there, Pearl is hurt, I don't know what to think, Pearl is hurt Prasad. Let's go, do something Prasad, for God's sake, do something."

The crowd saw that the newly weds were too intimate. Prasad put his hand around his new bride and took off with her.

SANDY COULD NOT think straight till she reached the hospital. People in the hospital were astonished to look at a newly wed bride running around in the hospital, holding her red sari in her hands. Prasad had managed to borrow a car from the marriage celebrations and asked the driver to get them to the hospital after informing Sneha's parents about the misfortune.

She reached the reception counter and asked for Sneha. She wanted to meet her as soon as possible. The doctor calmed her down before she could meet her. When she entered the room, she saw a peaceful sleeping Pearl in the bed, so very vulnerable. Except for the saline and the shiny plastic tubes running over her body, she seemed almost normal, just sleeping like a baby. She kneeled by her. Her head was bandaged with white mesh-like bandages. The doctors told her that there was a crack in her skull as she hit a concrete blocker and severe blood clot; hence there was little chance she could survive. After an hour or so, they would transfer her to a normal ward. She wanted to hug her Pearl and kiss her forehead, but she was afraid she was going to hurt her. She sat by her bedside, she wanted Prasad to be by her side, but only one person was allowed into the ICU.

She sat there crying silently and prayed to God like never before. When Sneha opened her eyes, she saw Sandy sitting by her side in the sari, which she had designed for her. She looked so pretty, her curls now came out of her tied up hair. She loved to look at her curls, "you have the cutest curls," she tried to smile at Sandy, but the tube would not let her do that. Surprised, Sandy looked up. She was happy she woke up; she called up the nurse, "Sneha what happened? How did you fell down the stairs?"

The nurse came running and started checking the monitors and noted down her pulse. "Her pulse has not yet returned to normal, I will call the doctor." The nurse ran away.

"Sandy, Satish…he wanted to talk to me." She took a deep breath, "I was trying to get away from him… I said I would talk to him later, but he wouldn't listen." Again, she took a deep breath, "I was trying to avoid him and I slipped." She gulped for a moment, "You are looking beautiful. Sorry I missed your marria…"

The doctor asked Sandy to leave, but Sandy wouldn't. She knew this was the last moment they were going to be together. She wanted to be with her. She caught her hand and gripped it, as if she would not let the God of death, take her away. Sneha gripped Sandy's hand softly, "my baby needs me." Her pulse monitor deafened Sandy. Sneha left this cruel, biased world.

NOW, SANDY AND Prasad live in the city in a humble house that they built and filled with love. It has been five years since Sneha's death and she has not been forgotten, still she lives in Sandy's heart. Sandy got up that morning, went to Sneha's photograph that was in her cupboard, "I am preparing Pooris today for your darling daughter."

She tied up her hair in a knot, kissed Prasad's forehead without waking him up, and went to the next room, "Sneha darling, wake up. I am preparing your favourite breakfast of Pooris. If you don't wake up, I will eat them all without leaving you anything."

"No, I will wake up Mummy. Where are my Pooris? I want them now."

"If you want them, get up, I will brush your teeth and then you can help me prepare the Pooris and we can finish them off before Papa wakes up."

"Nooo! I want Papa to eat the Pooris also."

"Really! My darling. You are such a sweetheart, just like your aunt Sneha."

"Mummy that is why we have the same name." She laughed and hopped out of the bed.

Sandy watched her five-year-old adopted daughter and never felt prouder. "I miss you Sneha. I miss you."

❂

2

A Fine Line

December 2006

MYTHILI WONDERED WHERE she was. She felt she was in the middle of a dark and never-ending labyrinth. She touched the rough stonewalls; they were cold – very cold. And suddenly she heard a familiar tone calling out, "Mythili. . . Where are you Mythili?" Her heart skipped a beat when the voice nostalgically took her to the memory lane of passion, her love – her life, Akash was calling her. She stumbled on a stone in that thick obscurity and fell into the wet sticky mud. She tried to lift herself up, but she could not. For a moment she thought she was in a quicksand, only, she was not going deeper into the mud. She felt she was unable to move as if a part of her was reluctant to get out of that place, that stinking place. The darkness scared her. . . yet she did not move.

Then again she heard Akash's voice, this time there was pain in his voice, "Mythili please come back. Give me my life back. Please." Tears burst out from her eyes, she gave a last effort and put in all her strength and pulled out her hands, at last she could move. She was free! She ran towards the voice and at the end of the tunnel, she could see the light. Walking out of the tunnel, she saw a huge abandoned building standing there like a moaning heart in the desert. And there in between the broken walls, he was! Akash stood there, still calling out for her. She stood in front of him, but still he could not see her. She shouted out to him, "Akash, I am here, just a feet away from you, can't you see me?" She tried to touch him and talk to him, but he was still calling out for her, she was invisible for him. Mythili's heart sank. . . He could not sense her. . . like always. She fell into a lump near his feet, crying. She looked up at his pain-filled eyes, "I love you Akash, I am sorry I hurt you, but I love you so very much." Just as if it was the magical word, he looked down smiling at me, "Mythili. . . there you are!" Mythili stood up and hugged him and they looked into each other's eyes for a moment. There was no change in his passionate green eyes. She kissed his lips and looked deep into his eyes, waiting. He smiled and kissed her back. Mythili was lost in his kiss, when suddenly she could not breathe. . . she struggled and now realised his kind features have now turned beastly. She tried to push him off, but she could not. She was imprisoned in his love, his kiss so strong that she was suffocating.

She felt scared, 'He is killing me!' Mythili was trying to take deep breaths, but she could not.

She heard him speak without moving his lips, "You said you could not breathe without me. . . but I am here now and still you are not able to breathe?"

She woke up and sat, feeling suffocated. It was a cool sunny morning. She sat there in her bed and looked around. Her son Bittu was sleeping beside her peacefully. She took a deep breath, 'That was just a dream.'

She fell back on the pillow and snuggled into the warm blanket, but she felt hot and kicked the blanket off of her, but her toes were chilled. She thought her dream felt too real, too close to death. Feeling the need for a cold splash, she got out of the bed, put on the slippers and walked over to the washbasin in the bathroom. She splashed cold water on her face and felt the piercing chillness on her skin. She could still feel Akash's warm breath over her, and his kiss. She looked up into the mirror; her lips looked red.

She stroked the edge of her lower lip with her finger, 'It has been a long time since these lips have been kissed.'

It has been six years and still she was obsessed about Akash and yearned for his kiss. 'I am no better than a teenage girl and I haven't learnt even a thing in these past ten years. How could I? This obsession, this passion for Akash is the only thing that makes me feel alive. I cannot imagine doing anything that is not a direct result of my love for him. And yet, I am guilty!' She sighed.

She put on a sweater, went to the kitchen, and prepared some coffee. She stood in the balcony, lost in the beauty of the place.

The evergreen cool and soft climate was the best part of Horsley Hills. Mythili got up early in the morning and took a deep breath of the cool and unpolluted air, and smiled. The sun made her skin glow with radiance and her softly curled hair shiny. She had a beautiful view from the balcony where she was standing. She could see the thick green hills standing tall next to each other that were being shaded by the clouds. Small streams curved along the hills. The best view was after a rainy day, when the still streams would reflect clouds like mirrors. Today was her day off from the yoga class that she taught in a gym in the hotel. She loved her job, teaching yoga and aerobics to tourists that come here to rejuvenate. She had developed various techniques to fit different age groups and different body sizes so that it was effective for their desired goals. She was one of the hotel's assets. She sat in the armchair putting her legs up on the wall, and was drinking hot coffee, when she heard Bittu running up to her.

"Good morning Mama," Bittu kissed her.

She put the coffee mug on the table beside her and hugged him, "Good morning Bittu. You woke up so early." She lifted him and made him comfortable on her lap.

"How can you forget Mama? Today is our picnic day! I want to be at the school bus first, so that I can save a seat for Moni…Monish."

Mythili laughed, "It's for Monica isn't it?"

"Mama! It is for Monish." Bittu looked violated. "Anyway, I will be ready in just a few seconds." His green eyes twinkled.

"Yes Bittu. And Mama will be ready too."

She looked at his bouncing silky brown hair as he ran off, 'Children these days! They want to grow up all too soon. He looks more and more like his dad everyday.'

AFTER DROPPING BITTU off at the school bus, Mythili went to the market place to buy some vegetables and some flowers to arrange in the house. She stood near the luscious green spinach when she looked around and saw those eyes, the green eyes looking fiercely at her. Mythili froze. She slowly turned around. 'It cannot be him.' She stood there aghast, 'How did he find me?' He was looking at her without a blink. She could not forget those green eyes and the intensity of those eyes that could bare the soul. He stood across her motionless, questioning her with his eyes. She saw that he was no longer the person she knew, his handsome face was wrinkled, his thin lips tightly sealed. The scar! How could she forget the scar she gave him? She had to act fast, as he was about to come towards her, a big truck came in between him, and Mythili ran from there. She knew she had escaped now, but not for long.

When she reached home, she did not know what to do. She wondered how he knew she was here. She did not even talk to her sister all these years. How could he possibly know where she was? Can she run again? When had she become such a coward? How did she become the woman she was now? Malicious and coward! There was nothing common between the woman she was ten years ago and the woman she is now. She knew she could no longer run now.

July 1997

MYTHILI WOKE UP and found Chetu's and Sweety's hands and legs on her. With a yawn, she gently pushed them aside so that she could get up and prepare for the aerobics class, she was teaching at a local gym. It was five o'clock in the morning, everyone was asleep and she hurried up to take a shower of cold water and run to the gym. Her class started at 6 a.m. and she was always there perfectly on time. Her class finished at around 8 a.m., when she hurried back home, got dressed up and helped her sister in getting the children ready for the school. She was to become an undergraduate in computers in a few months.

Standing silently by her sister's side, Mythili was packing lunch for herself, "*Akka I* want money for paying my exam fee."

Her sister looked at her with a smirk on her face, "Why, you are earning a good deal of money in that gym of yours, why do you need my help?"

"They will pay the money a bit late, I will give you back the money when I get my salary, but today is my last day to pay my exam fee." All the time she was talking to her sister, she kept looking down at the floor. She hated asking her sister for money.

"Ok, I will give you money this time, but be careful with your money from now on. Give me the money back when you get your salary."

"I will." Mythili looked at her sister and quickly looked down.

"I know you are my little sister and I should not take money from you, but I have to take care of two kids out of the small budget that my husband brings home. I am tired of taking care of so many people around the house." Her sister took out the money from her cupboard and gave it to her.

"I understand." She took out the money and carefully put it in her purse. That really hurt Mythili, 'If only I could complete my studies, I would get a decent job, then I could have lived in a hostel gladly.' But then, her sister was her only family. Probably, even then she would not go away.

Just then Chetu and Sweety came running to her, "*Pinni* let's start off, or else we will be late for school." Their school was a few blocks away and she would walk them to the school and catch a bus there to her college, which was some distance away. She bade them goodbye, but Chetu came back, "*Pinni* don't worry about what mom said to you. When I grow up, I will earn a lot of money and I will take care of you."

Mythili hugged him and kissed him on his forehead, "I am sure you will my Chetu, I am sure you will." Mythili loved both the children very much. Looking at her watch, she ran off as she was late for the bus. When she reached the bus stop, the bus had just left. "Oh no! It's Mr. Sharma's class. He won't allow me inside the class if I get late. She stood there waiting for the bus. 'It's no use waiting for the bus; I cannot miss the most important class of the semester.'

She looked across the street. It was Rishika's Scooty standing outside her gate. 'She could lend it to me for today. Rishika does not have classes on a Saturday.' She went to Rishika, explained to her that it was an emergency and took the Scooty. Rishika lent the bike to her because she knew Mythili would not ask unless it was absolutely necessary. Thanking Rishika profusely, she started off to her college.

Mythili was driving fast through the Minister Road, which generally was without much traffic at that part of the day. A few kilometres ahead, two men were tying a banner welcoming the Prime Minister; they were nearly finished when a gale from the Hussain Sagar Lake hit the banner and let it loose. Just then, Mythili was passing by and the wobbly banner hit her face and she hardly had time to stop the bike. She pulled the breaks, but the Scooty slid falling to the side and threw Mythili to the side. Mythili was trying to get up and move safely to the side of the road, but she was still dazed. Suddenly, a black car appeared from the street on the right, with thunderous music. The men who were just climbing down the wooden ladders were shouting, but their voices were too low for the person in the car to hear and the car's music was too loud. Mythili thought it was the last day of her life and closed her eyes. The car stopped in a screeching halt and the tyres burned their marks on the road. When Mythili heard the car halt, she opened her eyes and felt dizzy, she saw a man with black eye shades getting down the car and running towards her. She was losing consciousness, when she felt two arms lifting her from the ground gently and opened her eyes, everything was blurry. She looked up at the man who was carrying her and all she could see were two beautiful green eyes looking down at her. She was never the same again.

AFTER A FEW hours, Mythili woke up and found herself in a hospital bed; Chetu and Sweety were by her side and hugged her when she opened her eyes. "*Pinni* we were scared. Don't ever drive a bike *Pinni*." Both ran to bring their mother to her. Mythili sat on the bed. She felt sore all over her body, she felt a cast on her left hand, and she guessed that was because of a fracture. Now when she saw her sister come towards her, she wished she was unconscious again. Her sister started lecturing her how reckless she has been, and that the accident costed the family heavily. Just then, Mythili was thankful that her brother-in-law came in and stopped her sister's rambling. But even when her sister was scolding her, all she could think of was about the person who helped her. Later, she knew from the nurse that the man's name was Akash and that he admitted her in the hospital, called her sister, paid the money, and went away when he heard she had no severe injuries. Her sister was told about the Scooty, which was immediately recovered by her brother-in-law. All Mythili could think was, she could not thank him. She thanked God for sending 'him' on time.

✧

THE COOL SEASON of September set in Hyderabad, life was running its course again after she totally recovered from the accident she had. She got a project in a computer company, E-Soft. Anxiously, she was climbing the stairs and she met her classmate, Roopa, and they were jumping with excitement when they found out the project they were working on, and how good the company was, "It's a cool company." They were giggling and were so excited that Mythili did not notice that she was dangerously near the edge of the steps. She slipped and she was about to fall, when a strong hand caught her by her waist and she gave a shriek, more surprised by the hand that held her than the thought of falling down. She closed her eyes tightly. And then she realised she did not fall down and smelt familiar cologne that was faintly tantalizing her. She had enjoyed its scent before, then suddenly the green eyes flashed before her and she opened her eyes……her heart skipped a beat; she saw the same deep intense green eyes. For a moment, she thought it was a dream. Though she did not know anything about him, he did not seem like a stranger to her. Somehow, the world turned greener and rosier in an instant. The summary of her whole life was only this moment.

The handsome saviour waved his hand before her eyes, "Are you alright? Madam! Do you often fall into trouble like this?" He smiled.

Mythili had never thought that a simple smile could be so devastatingly beautiful. Then she recovered and stood aside, away from the steps, "Thank you for saving my life again." She felt embarrassed.

"Saving beautiful princesses is a knight's duty, anytime madam, anytime. But be careful. I might not be always around."

Mythili smiled. Her heart was beating unbearably fast.

"You were not really in any danger, I was just kidding. But you were in a semi-conscious state. How did you recognise me?" He looked straight into Mythili's eyes.

Smiling nervously Mythili blurted out, "I recognised your eyes."

"My eyes? Oh! But of course." He smiled mysteriously at Mythili.

"I did not get your name? Mythili questioningly blinked though she knew his name.

"Forgive my bad manners, I am Akash... Akash Choudhary. And I know you are Mythili Naidu. How are you feeling now? Any side effects of the accident? Of course not, the doctor said you were completely alright."

"Please call me 'Mythili'. Yes, there was pain for a few days and my fracture, but other than that I am perfect. And this is Roopa, she is my classmate and we are very excited about our project in such a good company. I have never been inside such a cool company and in my excitement I did not see I was near the edge of the steps."

"Yes I could see that, but be careful. Hello Roopa. Good to meet you."

"Hello, thanks for safely taking my friend to the hospital. She told me about the accident and how you helped her."

"Oh! No need to thank me. I did what any other person would do. So you are in the company for the project. Are you doing MBA or something?"

"Roopa and me, we are doing our B.Sc. in computers. We are here for the project for one month."

"Oh ok, you do look young for MBA, it's just that I am doing my project in MBA here. I guess I will see you around. Now I am late. Take care. I will take leave my lady." He bowed with his hand on his chest and went away, but his magic stayed on. He looked like a young movie star. Not everyone has that charm of a pied piper! Mythili watched him go and felt her heart warming slowly.

"Hmmm! Someone is totally flying in the dreams here," teased Roopa.

"Who is flying in the dreams? He saved me two times. So that is the reason I am looking at him. No subject is undeserving for you to tease me. I will also get a chance to tease you."

"No chance."

"We will see about that Paroo."

"Hey! Don't reverse my name."

"Paroo, Paroo, Paroo..."

"Youu...I will call you 'ithym' then..."

"It sounds cool! I have no problem with it, Paroo."

"I will kill you..." Roopa ran after her and she ran off to get away from Roopa, still calling her 'Paroo'.

Unknown to them, Akash was watching them through a glass slit on the adjacent room. Something about Mythili tingled his heart, her innocence, her unassuming attitude, and definitely like many girls of her age, she didn't know how good looking she was. Her glowing eyes, her pink chubby cheeks, her vulnerability, somehow it had a sexy look. Akash smiled, he was going to have some fun this month till they were together. He knew she was smitten. He too liked her.

He would bump into the friends once or twice in the cafeteria, sit with them, fight with Roopa, and give more attention to what Mythili had to say, which would make Mythili feel special and she was slowly falling for him. He asked Mythili to teach him a few computer basics so that he would directly learn some of the more modern languages and save time. Mythili readily agreed. As unassuming as she was, she knew Akash was only using it as a pretext to meet her alone without Roopa. Mythili felt adventurous for the first time in her life. She was alive when Akash was around. For once in her life, she could forget her problems and live for the moment. She enjoyed every minute she spent with him, his easy nature, sense of humour, and caring nature.

Akash would bring his laptop so that they could work in the office cafeteria, drinking cool drinks, eating anything in the cafeteria, and chatting for a while. But all the fun aside, Mythili thought Akash was very smart. When they were doing programs, he would be extremely serious about the work. It was like working with a totally different person. He would easily learn whatever she told him and if he would get a problem, he would work on it till he got it. This changed the total outlook for Mythili. She also began focusing on the project and her project manager was very happy with her work. The whole month passed by as if it was just a minute. Mythili dreaded the day when she had to say goodbye, though they would be in touch, it was not enough. It was now difficult for her even to imagine one day without seeing him. What's a sunflower without a sun?

✧

IT WAS THE last day of their project work and one day before the day of Dipawali. Mythili and Roopa were giving finishing touches to the project when a bald man came and started talking to them. His spectacles were thick and they made him look weird, every moment of his eyes were magnified for everyone to look at. He was one of the workers who had been in the company since its establishment. Chewing beetle leaves as always, he smiled at the two girls with his red-stained teeth, "So Roopa, it seems it's the last day of your project. Did you two girls do any work or you are just here for fun?"

Irritated Roopa looked at him, "We completed our project one week before the stipulated time Mr. Seshadri. The CEO looked at it and he is quite pleased with us."

"You will go nowhere with that anger of yours, Roopa," he smiled coolly again and the foul smell of the pan sickened Mythili and on impulse she waved her hand to wave off the foul smell. This irritated Seshadri and with discontent in the tone he talked to Mythili, "Roopa at least would work some of the time, you are always running around that Akash. I never saw you work at all. If you dream that by flirting with Akash, you can become the owner of this company; you don't have a clue what you are up against."

"Owner of the company? What are you talking about?" asked Mythili totally baffled.

“Oh! You should try acting for movies or serials. As if you didn’t know Akash is the son of the owner of this company, that too, the only son! Very smart! Anyway I am just an old loyal employee of the company. What do I care? Mr. Choudhary is smart enough to handle you.”

Seshadri went away shaking his head, smiling with content and thought, ‘She really didn’t know!’ Then turned around to look at Mythili again, she was in shock now. She stood looking at Roopa. Seshadri again walked towards them, “You really didn’t know then. . . may be it’s Akash who is playing games with you, hahaha…he was always a naughty boy, if you know what I mean.” Seshadri had his last word. This day was not one of his boring days, he was having fun and he knew there will be amusing days ahead.

Mythili did not believe Seshadri about what he said about Akash playing with her. But what was she thinking? Why had she so senselessly and hopelessly fallen in love with Akash? She knew he was a rich kid even though he did not tell her he was the future owner of the company. Then she felt a pang, did everyone in the office think about her the same way that Seshadri thought? Everyone knew about Akash and everyone saw them working in the cafeteria. Did Akash too think that she was flirting with him because he was rich and owned a big company? She felt everything go hazy. She could not think straight. She turned to Roopa, “I need to cool down Roopa; I will leave early today and go and sit in the temple for some time.”

“Mythili, don’t feel bad. You know Seshadri has a foul mind matching his foul breath. Don’t take him seriously. I too did not know Akash was the son of Mr. Choudhary.”

“Yes I know that, otherwise, you would have told me and I would not have been insulted. Anyway, sorry I am leaving you in the middle, but I think you can handle it. Bye.” Mythili left even before Roopa said bye.

✧

JUST AN HOUR later or so, Akash came looking for Mythili, "Good morning Roopa. Where is Mythili? Is she talking to Mr. Choudhary?"

"You mean your dad? No! She went away for today." Roopa looked at him scornfully and started doing her work.

"You seem angry, just chill Ms. Chilli and tell me what happened?" Akash blocked her keyboard.

"Take off your hands. You want others to insult me too? I am not a softy like Mythili."

Akash was taken aback, "Insult?"

Roopa told Akash what had happened and how Seshadri had talked to her. Akash smiled, "All this! Just because I am the owner's son. Roopa...no one can change narrow-minded people. Just because such people talk nonsense, it does not make the truth distorted. Never take such kind of people seriously, or else only we will suffer. Now, what do I do? I can't even call her at her home; I guess I will need to wait till tomorrow."

That evening Akash sat in his terrace on the soft-cushioned swing and looked up into the sky, he was feeling very uneasy. He wanted to meet Mythili and knowing how sensitive Mythili was, she would definitely be crying right now. How he wished to be with her, it was a beautifully-lit night. Akash got excited, 'Idea! That would surely cheer Mythili.'

THE NEXT DAY, Mythili and Roopa gave a presentation of the project and everyone was pleased with their work. It was late evening before both the friends spent some time in the cafeteria, saying cheers with their coffee cups. Just then Akash came to their table and looking at Mythili, he said "Can I join you?"

"Akash, please do sit. We don't know when we will meet again. This is our last day at this place." Mythili seemed distant, but courteous.

Akash turned to Roopa who looked at him puzzled, "Hi Roopa," then he turned to Mythili, "I heard what happened yesterday. I guess you must be hurt. Don't feel bad about the trash he spoke."

"About that! I forgot. Just because he says something, it does not mean it is true. Anyhow, today is my last day of the project. I won't be in this company – at least for some time. I need to complete my masters before joining this company," smiled Mythili.

After an awkward pause, Akash questioned, "We will still be friends, right?"

At this question, Mythili looked away, "Of course!" She tried to look busy as if she wanted to find something in her bag.

Looking at her uneasiness, Roopa said, "Come on, let's go Mythili. It is getting late." Then she turned to Akash, "Good bye Akash, we had a good time. Bye, see you around."

"Bye Roopa, sorry for teasing you so much." Akash looked disappointed.

"Tease me! You are quite mistaken my friend. Bye."

Akash sat in his car thinking, he felt empty. The way Mythili answered, it seemed now they would never meet each other. He could not bear to think of it. 'She is my friend. How can I be happy without meeting her? I already miss her terribly.' He looked right, where she generally waited for the bus. She stood there deeply lost in her own thoughts, 'She never looked so sad.' He had to do something. He drove to that bus stop and called out for Mythili.

Mythili was surprised, "What happened? Why are you still here? Didn't you go home?"

"Get into the car; I need to show you something."

"I am getting late Akash, I am sorry." Mythili hated herself for saying that.

"Please, just this once. I want to show you something. I know you will really love what I am about to show you." Akash looked at her pleadingly.

Mythili smiled, "Ok sir. But I need to be home by nine o'clock. Or my sister will be cross with me."

Akash smiled, "Don't worry, you will be home exactly by 8:59 p.m. madam."

"Really! What is so special about what you are showing me?" She sat on the passenger seat.

Akash was delighted, he kicked on the accelerator and the car jumped forward. He drove coolly through the traffic and small roads with ease and Mythili felt him to be a totally different person while driving. She felt his passion for cars that he so often talked about. He loved driving. She felt Akash was his complete self while driving. It felt like second nature to him. In half an hour or so, just as the evening became calmer and duskier, they reached the outskirts of the city. Akash took a sharp turn and they were running along a mud road that Mythili felt sure was not known to many people. There was thick vegetation around and she could see no one as far as her view went. She turned to Akash, "What is this mysterious place? What do you want to show me?"

Akash was concentrating on the road ahead to avoid bumps, but smiled, "You will see, my lady." Mythili always felt good when he treated her like a princess and called her 'my lady'. She felt excited as to what lied ahead. She felt like a pirate in search of some hidden treasure.

Akash stole glances at her once in a while; he felt Mythili was just like a kid. Everything was a big adventure for her. She felt everything was priceless as if she had been jailed her whole life and did not know anything about life. He could hardly resist being fond of her. She was like a princess locked in a dungeon. The moonlight from the windows fell on her cheeks and she really looked like a fairy. Her dark eyelashes were like a painter's brush strokes that moved swiftly whenever she blinked and she blinked so often. When he knew how she managed her life, her gym classes, her sister's children, her education, he was impressed by her toughness even though she looked so vulnerable. He could not imagine what he would do without his parents and no money for his education. He respected her for he has never met anyone like that. He discovered a different side of himself, he began enjoying little things in life. He acknowledged his respect for his parents in simple things, his mother was very pleasantly surprised one day when he bought her some flowers just like that, her favourite Lilies. He even became obedient to his father, which pleased him immensely. Because of Mythili, he knew the importance of life, and its little things. He often questioned himself, did he love her? But he brushed the idea away. He did not think it was really so.

As they climbed a small hill, it was very dark. There were some fireflies here and there. There were those little noises from the beetles that called on each other. Mythili felt her fingers go cold. It was cold and she closed the window. Akash did the same. And then they reached the end of the road and the car stopped. Akash turned the engine off, "We are here, come let's get out of the car."

Both of them got out and Akash took Mythili's hand, this quickened her pulse. He covered her eyes and took her a little further. It was dark, but the small lights from the car guided them and there a big rock that was exactly like the benches in the parks. They settled there on the rock. Akash could feel Mythili's warm breath on his forearm. "Now it's time for you to open your eyes my lady," and he removed his hand from her eyes.

When Mythili opened her eyes, she thought she was in a wonderland. The whole city of Hyderabad, with all its fancy lights, was looking gorgeous and tiny. And on top of that, it was Deepavali and the firecrackers made the sky look colourful. The rockets went up and burst out into different shapes and colours, some burst as fountains and disappeared and some burst and twinkled in the sky for sometime in multicolour. Mythili clapped her hands, "It's so beautiful Akash. I never thought that such a place could even exist. Wow! It is so beautiful. I love it, I love it."

Akash watched her stand up and jump. She enjoyed it. He knew she would love this view, "I knew you would love it."

Mythili came back and sat beside him, "How did you know about this place? I do not think many people know about this place." She blinked.

"Oh! That is a long story and it happened a long time ago. I was in intermediate and one day my dad and mom were out of town and by chance I got the keys of a car. I wanted to impress my girlfriend." Akash was lost in the talk, but Mythili's face suddenly became gloomy, her smile vanished. Akash continued, "So I asked her to sneak out of the house and we drove out. I accidentally found this place while driving out with her and my friends and fooling around. I just fell in love with this place and thought my girl would also like this place. But do you know what she said when I brought her here?" Akash turned to look at Mythili and to his surprise, she burst into tears, "Why what happened? You were laughing just now."

"Nothing! So why did you bring me here? To tell me about your love life. You should have brought your girlfriend here. Why did you bring me here?" Mythili was irritated.

"Are you jealous or something?" Akash felt naughty.

"Why would I be? I am not your girlfriend or anything like that."

"Hmmm! You need not be a girlfriend to be jealous you know, but you look cute when you are angry. I should make you angry more often."

"I am not cute."

"Oh yes you are!" and on impulse Akash kissed her lips.

Mythili jumped back, "You have a girlfriend!"

Akash felt it very amusing. He pulled Mythili closer to him, "No… that is what I was telling you. When I brought her here, she hated it and started complaining on and on what a crap of a place it was and it was enough for me to break that relation. She had no idea what beauty was. And that was a long time ago. I don't have a girlfriend now."

This seemed to cool down Mythili, she was feeling flustered and did not know what to do. She felt embarrassed and looked down, away from him. Akash lifted her chin, "I have never met a woman like you. I cannot think of anything else when you are standing in front of me. You are so beautiful in this moonlight, just like a fairy." Mythili looked up into his eyes, she felt warm and she wanted to break all bonds. She wanted to be in his arms, feeling his body. His warm breath washed her face.

She smiled, "I am sorry. I acted so inappropriately."

"My lady, you have acted most appropriately till now. You truly are a princess," he locked his hands around her, "I am sorry Seshadri said all those things to you. I knew how hurt you must be. So I thought this will cheer you up." Mythili stood there like a stone. She did not know what to say or do. She did not know where all this was going. Then he removed his hands around her waist and caught her by her hands, "I am sorry Mythili, I kissed you. It was not my plan, cross my heart. You looked so beautiful and it was an impulse. I am sorry." Akash was about to leave her hands when Mythili caught him and kissed him. Akash was surprised at her passion and kissed her back. None of them knew what they were doing. At that time, everything other than that moment seemed like an oblivion...

As they lay there in silence and now that each had come back to the reality, everything felt wrong. Every thought that came felt sinful, every word they wanted to say felt wrong. Like so many awkward pauses between a word and a deed, they paused looking away from each other. The sky was still lit with rocket crackers that were as bright as ever, if not more brighter. The bombs blasted everywhere in the city and both the hearts burst out with the fear of losing each other and both of them felt the heart beat so loud that they worried the other might hear it.

Akash felt he did a mistake, 'I should not have brought her here. How would I make it right? What would I say or do that would make everything right? Did I love her? May be, may be not. But she was amazing.' He could not shake off the sweet moments, the way she quivered when he touched her waist, the way her muscles tensed up when he stroked her legs, the way she was lost in ecstasy when he kissed her. She looked happy, she felt so strong yet gentle. She was beautiful. Akash brought himself back from the memories, 'What am I thinking? She is not a spoilt brat to fool around. What does she expect from this? She hardly talks to any guy. But one thing is for sure, she loves me truly. She really loves me! But she is a big girl, she knows I did not promise her anything; but is she? I do not know what to say or do. What should I do? I don't want to hurt her.' He was confused now.

Mythili was scared now. She has given herself totally to him. She loved him with all the passion in the world. She did not know she was capable of loving a person so much that she was willing to give herself away in return of nothing. She loved him, soulfully. Surprisingly, in contrast to her belief of having a physical relation with only the husband, she did not feel she did anything wrong, 'I have never felt so happy! I really do love him. Does he love me? May be he loves me, we made love. But he is so silent,' Mythili looked at the perplexed expression on Akash's face. 'Oh God! He thinks it's a mistake. He does not love me. What do I do? I cannot show my face to him. Our friendship is ruined. I have to say something.' Mythili turned to him, "Akash let's go. This was a mistake." To her horror, Akash looked relieved. It took all the strength she had, to control herself from crying.

Akash stood up from the ground and gave her hand, "Let's go." He was scared to say anything else.

Both of them sat in the car just the same way that they came, but the innocence was now lost, as if it never existed. The tender smile was gone. Mythili knew at that moment that she had lost a treasure that she never noticed she had – her happiness. She knew she would never be the same again. She had read in so many books and heard in so many movies that sentence, *never the same again*, but she now knew the real meaning of it and it hurts, a thorn had slipped into her heart and she felt it would never come out. While his smooth hands passed over her, she felt she was his slave. When she kissed him and lay on his chest for a second, she felt she owned him, he was her Man. Was she imagining it? Her mind went numb. There were too many questions and no answers. She just looked ahead, the street lights passed by, the traffic passed by, people passed by, everything was the same. . . she was not – she was never going to be the same.

Akash looked nervously at her. She seemed different now. She looked like a stranger to him now. Her eyes looked lifeless; he saw fear in her eyes for the first time. Her cheeks no longer blushed with the timid smile. What had he done? What can he do now to make it right? He could no longer tolerate the silence. He turned left to talk to Mythili when she turned to him and asked him to stop.

Akash looked at her questioningly. Mythili repeated, "Stop the car Akash, I need to get down here." He stopped the car and was about to say something when Mythili got off the car and already closed the door and was about to leave. Akash got out of the car and ran to the other side and called her, "Mythili wait." She stopped. He continued, "I don't know what to say or how you are feeling, but...."

"Akash, please do not say anything. I know this was a mistake. No need to worry. I will be fine. Bye." Mythili started to walk.

"You have my number, will you. . . will you call me?" Akash stuttered.

Mythili stopped, took a deep breath, "What for? We ruined a perfect friendship." Akash did not expect this. He was dumbstruck when Mythili turned, she was bursting into tears. She came near him, "I love you with all my heart Akash. From the moment I saw you, I had no choice but to fall in love with you." Mythili savoured his aura; she only had this memory to live with. She looked into the mystic green eyes, but looked away as if she was scared of falling in love again. She hurried away before Akash could speak.

Akash stared after her gaunt figure vanishing in the shadows. He wanted to reach out for her, embrace her, and make her his. But something stopped him. He knew this was not meant to be. Yet, his heart ached for her. May be he loved her.

IT HAS BEEN over two months and looking at the winter sky from the terrace of her house, Mythili rubbed her chilled fingers to make them warm. In this cold night, all she could think of was the time she spent with Akash – that beautiful night. She desired for one more kiss, just one. That day of Deepavali was the last day she talked to him, neither called each other. Mythili thought that as timed passed by, her pain may lessen. She felt the same way when she lost her mother when she was fifteen. The emptiness and pain seemed intolerable, but over the time it lessened and she had come and lived with her sister. Life went on; she became so busy with her life that it numbed her pain. She tried to do the same. She was taking extra classes of aerobics and gym; she was focusing all her time into studying and doing household work for her sister. She was exhausted, and still she forced herself.

Roopa had seen this drastic change in her and asked her the reason and whether this was linked with Akash in anyway. She excused herself saying either she was too busy or too tired and just wanted to relax at home. Roopa knew that something was wrong. Mythili used to be a girl who laughed easily for even a silly joke. She always enjoyed solving problems in the class. She would help anyone in the class with problems in their subjects, but not anymore. She would just slip out of the class now. She did not talk or laugh much. Roopa wondered what happened. Mythili was avoiding her and she saw that she was really working on the subjects, but it seems she was not able to concentrate much. She was not that active in the class. And she always looked sad as if in some pain all the time. Roopa felt talking with Akash would be the best thing to do and called up his number to meet him. Roopa thought Akash was pleasantly surprised when she called him. They decided to meet near the same office they met.

Roopa reached there earlier and waited for Akash wondering what to ask him. When Akash arrived in his bike, she was surprised to see that even Akash seemed different. Not tired or sad, just different. Not his mischievous self that he generally was around her, teasing her. He looked more formal and down to earth. He just came to her and said good evening and smiled. Roopa was now sure that the same thing was bugging Akash and Mythili.

She decided to ask, "Hello Akash. How are you?"

"I am fine. How are you?"

"I am fine. Let me get down to business."

"I didn't know you had a business of your own Roopa!"

"Ha ha, very funny." Roopa made a sarcastic face. "The reason I wanted to meet you was about Mythili."

"Mythili? Why, what happened to her? We lost touch. Deepavali was the last day we met." Roopa saw that Akash was concerned.

"Nothing serious. It's just that she does not seem her usual self. She looks sad. I thought you might know something." Roopa somehow did not expect an honest answer.

"Really!" He seemed downcast. "I don't know the reason. But can I do something, anything to make her feel good again?"

"I don't know what to do. That was the reason I wanted to meet you to see if you could help me out. She always seems much happier with you around. You make her laugh, can't you just call her or something?"

"Call her. . . I don't know whether she would like that?"

"Ok Akash, let me talk straight to the point. It is no use beating around the bush. I feel strongly that this has something to do with you. And I want you to fix it. She is hurt because of you, I am sure of it. She already has a hundred problems to deal with; she does not need another one because of you. I hope you make it right. I just wanted to say that." Roopa looked at Akash for any signs of defiance, but he did not. He just sat there thinking. She felt she could do nothing more, "Bye Akash."

"Bye Roopa. Thank you. Mythili has a good friend looking out for her."

Roopa smiled, "You would do the same for your best friend." And she went away.

Akash thought 'Would I?' She was one of his good friends in such a short time. She was a person he could relate to so easily and yet one moment destroyed it all. He missed having long talks with her about politics, nature, and everything under the sky. He missed having coffee in the cafeteria. He missed shopping with her. He missed her very much. Akash decided it was time to talk to her. Ask for her forgiveness and try to make things right. He decided he would meet her near her college the next day.

The next day he waited in his car outside her college. It was about four o'clock in the evening and an exodus of young girls walked out in the most vibrant colours, laughing and smiling, gossiping, and ridiculing lecturers. It was a beautiful sight, more beautiful than the sunset. Just then Akash sighted Mythili, she really looked different. The smile on her face completely vanished. There was no reminiscence of happiness in her. He got out of the car and started towards her. She looked lost in her thoughts. When she saw Akash, her smile found its way home. Involuntarily, she ran towards him saying bye to her friend. Seeing her coming towards her, Akash stopped just a few feet away from the car.

She reached him puffing and suddenly she caught his hands, "I knew you would come back to me. I knew you would miss me. I knew you loved me." She looked like a child; Akash did not know what to say. Now he could not become the reason for the smile to vanish away again. He forgot what he wanted to say to her *all that has happened* these two months. He wanted to tell it gently, but as she caught his hands, he forgot all about it. The exquisite night felt just like yesterday. He could still feel her smooth warm skin. He just stood there looking at her dark black eyes.

Some girls passed by, "Oh, look at them, these days Romeos come in cars, is it? All the girls laughed at them teasingly.

"Let's go," Akash held the door open for Mythili to get in.

Excited, she got into the car. In just a period of second, she was dreaming of forever together. Dreams are so alive and kicking when one is in love, but when one loses that, dreams turn hopeless and trap one into a never ending tunnel of despair – and yet we dream of that special someone. Then Mythili realised she had spoken too soon. She was wishing him to love her back so desperately that she thought he only came back out of love. She got scared. When she saw Akash sit in the driver's seat, her heart was filled with anguish. He looked troubled. She sat in silence. He sat in silence, just driving. She did not know where they were going and she did not care. Akash drove the car around Necklace Road and stopped it under the shade of a tree. They sat in silence dreading what the other would say.

At last, Akash took a deep breath, "Mythili I wanted to talk to you. I am really sorry for that night. I don't know what came over me. I should have. . ." He could not speak. Akash turned to her side, "all I wannaaa. . . Please do not cry. I could not forgive myself all these months. I could not stop thinking about you. Please do not cry." Akash panicked.

Mythili turned red and burst into tears. She had not cried even once in the last two months. She had buried her dreams, but now the dead dreams came alive when she saw those deep green eyes and the concern on his brow. She did not realise how much she loved him till the moment she saw him standing there before the college gate. She thought her dreams would become true forever, but the thought of losing him again made her lose her mind, it made her crazy. She felt she was losing control of her life which she worked so hard to build.

She could not take it anymore, "If you wanted to just say goodbye, you could have left me alone. Why did you come back? That night I gave you not only myself, but my soul too. Have you ever done that Akash, did you? So when you ask for forgiveness, can you give back my soul too? Do you know how empty I felt these two months? I could only become complete with you, don't you know that? Why have you returned Akash, what else is left in me that you have returned to take away?" She looked straight into his eyes.

Akash could hear his heart beat now. He never thought he could hurt someone so deeply. He knew he could not make things better. The only thing he could do was not do further damage, but he was not strong enough. At that moment, with passion-stricken heart he hugged her and kissed her. He missed her very much. He thought he could never let go off her, "Mythili I missed you so much. I cannot see you cry. I want you to smile all the time." He kissed her again and Mythili gave in. She knew now, there was no turning back – but she still went ahead.

Akash still felt guilty. He did not tell her the whole truth. She was like the crystal that shone so brightly that Akash could not let go off, but she was not the diamond that he could wear on the ring.

December 1998

AKASH WAS IN his cabin, with the letters Managing Director stuck to it, when the call came from the secretary.

"Sir, a Ms. Mythili wants to meet you. She says it is very urgent. Should I send her in?"

Akash did not understand why she came to the office. They always met at her place. What was so urgent that she could not call him or wait till they meet that evening? "Ok, send her in."

On that busy day, people could see a pretty woman in a black sari rushing towards their Managing Director's cabin. She was new here. They hoped she was a new girl joining the office, but her manner did not seem so. The way she opened the door with sheer force and the look of anger made people wonder. She did not look like an interviewee; she looked more like a bully.

Akash knew just by looking at Mythili that something was wrong. She never looked this angry, "What was so urgent that you could not wait till evening? What happened? You look different – angry."

"Angry? Then what the hell should I be? You were engaged for a year and you did not even care to mention that to me! You brute!... How could you do this to me?" Mythili was too angry to care that it was not in her nature to curse. She felt her world was ending and she was thrown into a whirlpool of deceit and betrayal.

Akash could not speak a word, but he was scared, "I know you are very angry right now. Please just calm down. Just sit."

"How can I calm down? You have kept me in dark for all these months. You did not care to enlighten me on such a simple truth that you are already engaged." Mythili's voice rose.

Flustered, Akash could only say, "I wanted to tell you, but it was too late by then."

This seemed to anger Mythili even more, "When were you thinking of telling me? When you were married and had two kids! What was I in your perfect family picture, your mistress?"

Her voice was rising with every word she said. Betrayal is a slow poison that becomes more lethal as it breeds with time. She was cheated for a year, a year for which she always thought she could sell her soul to get it back. All that she yearned for in her life, she had, but now everything seems to dissolve into thin air. It was a conjuror's trick, an illusion, and the worst thing was she had let herself get tricked. Yes, she always felt it was too good to be true, she felt like Eve in the Garden of Eden with her Adam, but that's it, it was only she and Akash in her world, no one else in the family were involved, she should have known it. And yet, she loved him, even this minute of disgust. She did not hear what Akash was saying; she just collapsed into the chair next to her, hands over her head. It was not only Akash's betrayal. . . her reluctance to see the situation as it was, had led her into the path of destruction. Akash never promised her anything.

She turned to Akash who was babbling and asked him, "What do I do now Akash? What am I supposed to do?"

Akash who was trying to convince her all this time, just stopped and sat on the chair by her side. He stared at her. Her sudden calmness, the way she composed herself again, it puzzled him. He took a deep breath, "For now, just go home. We will talk in the evening."

With strained eyes that were fighting to stop the tears, Mythili looked into Akash's eyes. She knew he was leaving her. With shock and hopelessness, she walked out of the office like a living corpse.

THAT EVENING, AKASH arrived at her house, a little late than he usually does. When she came back home, she did not cry, she did not plan her future, she just sat in a kind of trance and stillness. She could only hold herself responsible for what happened. She wanted to curse Akash, but she could not. She loved him too much to do that. She could not forget that he had saved her life, physically and emotionally too. When she heard footsteps on the stairs, she knew it was Akash.

Akash's stride was slow and doubtful. He had decided, but how could he say that to her. He could not break the engagement, he liked Nisha. His family liked her too. Nisha's father and his father have started a new business together as partners and if he breaks his engagement, they would not be able to stand back on their own again. Crores of money was involved and lots of people worked in their company. All that would become dust if he behaved otherwise. He once thought he loved Mythili, he thought he could work it all out. But since he has met Nisha, everything turned different. She was more mature than him in the matters of business and emotions. Somehow, he had become dependent on her. For his career and life, Nisha would act as a catalyst and she made him dream of bigger dreams, going global, and be a celebrity. The last year had been a roller coaster ride for him. He had achieved recognition in business that no other person of his age and experience could have achieved and Nisha was the main reason.

But he could not say all this to Mythili. That day near the college, the way she had said with innocence in her eyes, "You have come back for me!" He could not say he was engaged. He loved her innocence, her child-like attitude, her simple beauty. He could not leave her. His weakness had made him a man he never dreamed he could be. When had he become such a shallow person, he questioned himself on and on with no answer. But now, he has decided – he has to leave Mythili.

He saw the door open and Mythili sitting in a chair near the door waiting for him. She was in the same black sari she was wearing in the morning in which she looked beautiful. Her silky long hair was only blacker than her sari, he always wondered how she would look with her hair coloured in browns or burgundy, but she always refused to let her hair dyed. She loved black and her eyes matched her hair. One of the reasons he could not let go off Mythili was that he could be himself with her and he could forget all the pressures of his life near her. She was a typical Indian girl and that was a difficult task. She was always patient, uncomplaining, unassuming, and was always there to listen to him. Nisha was tough, she was a perfectionist and expected perfection out of everyone around her, especially him. He was always on his toes with her around.

He tiptoed towards Mythili and sat by her side and touched her hand, Mythili startled and looked at him. She jerked out from the chair and stood facing him, suppressing her anger, spoke in a low but stern tone "Don't touch me!" Akash looked at a totally different side of Mythili, but what else could he expect?

"When would you have told me? May be never. How could you do this to me? What have I done to deserve this from you?"

"I am sorry Mythili. I should have told you long before. The day I came to the college, I wanted to tell you that I was engaged, but the way you reacted, tongue-tied me. I could not say anything to you and I never had the courage to tell you the truth."

"Truth! Let me tell what the truth is. You are a selfish person. When did you become like this? You are cheating not only me and that girl, but also yourself. How could you live cheating like this?"

"I know I cheated you. I cannot say anything but sorry. I am really sorry to hurt you like this. I really care for you. But I have no choice." Akash paused.

"I know you have made your choice. It was just a matter of time before you came to a conclusion. Don't act as if you are guilty. You have no remorse of what you have done. Come out with it. Say what you have come here to say."

"I am getting married this January. (He paused) I am sorry Mythili. You have the right to say anything you want to say. You can curse me as much as you want and I know that would not even make up to what I have done. But I cannot see you anymore Mythili."

Akash hesitated to look at Mythili. She looked pale and sick, but he had to go on, "There is a lot at stake here, families and people. I cannot disappoint all of them. My fiancé's family and our family are partners of a firm that we have recently set up. If I do my duty towards you, lot of people will suffer and I will be the cause of their wrath. But if chose the other path, I will do a lot of good to so many people and selfishly my family too. So I am ready to become an object of your wrath."

Akash looked at Mythili; her sweet lips were shivering with the pain of her breaking heart. He knew she loved him very much, may be more than anyone else in the world. He only hoped she would forgive him with time."

"What am I supposed to do without you Akash?"

"Time is the best healer Mythili. With time you will slowly forget me and you will find your true love soon. Any guy would be lucky to have you."

Mythili smiled sarcastically, "Why cannot you be the lucky guy then?"

"You know the answer for that. Have faith Mythili, you are a smart, intelligent woman. You have become what you are without anyone's help. After some time, may be you would even think I was not the right person for you and everything happened for a good reason."

To this Mythili gave a smirk. Akash did not mind, he went on "I will not be available to you emotionally, but I want to take care of you. I will take care of you financially till you get back on your feet. I will transfer some amount of money to your bank account. That wil..."

"Get lost! Get out of my house. Is there anything else other than your money that you care about? I don't want your bloody money. Be happy with Nisha. You are actually scared that I will tell your dirty little secret to her and that is why you are here, isn't it? You are here to shut my mouth with money. No need to pay me, you beast! Get out! Never ever come back again because, if you come back again I will kill you. GET OUT!"

"Mythili! I don't know what to say."

"No need to say anything, leave my house." Mythili turned away from him. Her heart was breaking into pieces. She had heard so many songs saying that the heart was breaking, but she now realised the pain in it and what it really meant. Whoever writes those songs? There is no way of describing a broken heart. Silently, she wept as she heard the faltering steps fade away. She would never see him again. She collapsed. The marble floor faced the wrath of her closed fists, Mythili cried out, "I hate you Akash. I hate you." But her heart resounded, *I Love You.*

A car with the stereo pumped up high passed by, with the song from the movie, *Dil Se*, "*Ishq par jor nahi, hai yeh woh atish ghalib, jo lagaye na lage, jo bhujaye na bhuje.*"

Passion is a fire that cannot be lit nor can be extinguished even if one wanted to.

March 2000

SOME PEOPLE CHANGE as fast as the time does, but some do not change though time runs past. Mythili belonged to the latter. She got a good job, invested all her time doing one activity or the other, tried meeting new people, but she remained the same woman that Akash had left one year ago. Sometimes she would go to her sister's house to meet Chetu and Sweety, but her sister would always bug her about getting married and would show a new profile of the prospective bridegroom every time. The only beautiful moment in her life now was the time she spent with Chetu and Sweety. Both were growing up fast and more mature everyday. Chetu would often ask her why she was not staying with them and that he missed her. Mythili joked that she cannot live with kids any longer and the hostel was full of girls of her age. She hated that working women's hostel, but it was safe there and she had very little time there to think of Akash.

The month when Akash got married, Mythili vacated the apartment that Akash had taken rent for her. She found this hostel and was staying there since then. Getting a job was a bit difficult, but by sheer luck she got a job in a reputed company (sometimes she thought Akash had something to do with, but she waved off the thought). She found some considerable amount of money in her account, but she did not touch it. She despised the money. It made her feel dirty. She considered donating the amount to someone, but was reluctant to do so. Her life took the routine course after a few months; she liked the new office and the people in her office. She spent her time with hostel friends, keeping her professional life, very professional. In no time, she became close with Parimila Rao, her roommate. They spent all the time together in and out of the hostel. On Sundays, Parimila spent time with her brother who used to pick her up. That was the only time when Mythili felt alone. She tried doing new courses and reading them, but she could not concentrate much. Parimila made her secure, she was a mature and strong person and if she wasn't around, that made the day worse for her.

One day when Parimila returned to the hostel room, she found Mythili crying and she knew that Mythili could not be left alone. From the next Sunday on, all three of them spent time together, Mythili, Parimila and her brother, Shashank. Soon they all turned out to be good friends, Mythili started liking Shashank. He was a good person and cared about Parimila deeply as if she was not his sister, but his own kid. After spending a month or two, Mythili thought that Shashank could make her forget the past. She thought she could still have hope. But she waved off her thoughts.

Shashank also liked Mythili and in due course, he started coming twice a week to the hostel just to see Mythili. Parimila first was surprised and then she noticed the change in her brother's eyes. After much thought, Parimila told him about Mythili's affair and how the guy had married someone else. She thought she was doing the right thing and told him that Mythili herself had told her and that she did not want Shashank to get hurt. Parimila resented the fact that her brother would like Mythili. Mythili was a good friend, but only to that…She did not deserve her brother!

But the minute Parimila told her brother, she realised she had broken his heart and then realised how deeply in love he was with her. But some words bury themselves deep in the heart, and echo from time to time. Shashank was not sure what he could do. He was confused and he stopped meeting or calling Mythili. When he did not come to the hostel for two weeks or so, Mythili asked Parimila the reason for his long absence. Parimila, who now was convinced the reason her brother and she grew apart was Mythili, closed her eyes for a moment to calm down, but it only served to magnify her anger. She opened her eyes and in a cold tone, she said, "Stay away from my brother. My brother deserves someone far better than you."

Mythili saw the hate in her eyes, 'When did she become a stranger?' She froze; she did not know what to do. Her mind was just blank. She sat on the bed like a lump. Her mind was still blank when she saw Parimila leave the room. She was now broken completely. She knew somewhere in the corner of her heart that Akash would desert her, but she never dreamt her friend would abandon her too. She stayed alone in the room till the darkness crept from her heart out in to the real world. As the day went to sleep, her head started pounding with headache and she needed some Dispirin. When she reached a medical shop near her hostel, she got more than Dispirin – she found Akash.

She was shocked to see Akash. He looked dishevelled and tired. He looked lost. He was almost unrecognisable. Akash did not even see her. He was just standing by her side and asked the druggist for a milk bottle and he faltered. Mythili was surprised to hear this, but sensed something was wrong. She did not know what to do. Akash was a mistake of her life. He was the reason she became all alone and any relation with Akash would only be a dead end. But when was her heart her's? "Hi Akash."

Akash froze. He stood there – still, for a moment. He recognised the voice, but he prayed it was not her. Mythili felt it like an eternity. At last, Akash turned around and smiled deliberately.

Mythili saw his swollen blood shot eyes. He looked as if he had not slept for many days, "Are you alright?" Akash didn't speak, he looked away and a tear shone in the corner of his eye. To make him feel better, Mythili looked at the milk bottle he was holding tightly and said, "Is it a boy or a girl?"

Akash relaxed a bit, "It's a boy. He is the cutest baby I have ever seen."

Mythili smiled, seeing Akash somehow made her forget about the betrayal. She had pictured Akash and herself living in a small home with a baby and she always figured the baby will have Akash's green eyes. She closed her eyes and pictured the baby and smiled, "The baby has green eyes like yours. Doesn't he?"

Akash was stunned, "Yes! How did you know that?"

"Somehow I knew that. I always pictured it like that – errr…….. in the past. You look troubled. How is your wife?"

Akash took a deep breath, "She is in heaven." He looked down trying to fight back tears.

"What! How? When did this happen? I am sorry! I should not have asked you all these questions." Mythili forgot all about the hate she felt for Akash the past year. It was only replaced by concern for the baby and Akash.

"You have not changed a bit Mythili. You are a good person. You still care for me. Do not care for me Mythili, I do not deserve it." He could not hold back his tears. "I need to go now. If you like, you can come by some time to my house. You can see the little guy. Bye." Akash did not wait for her reply. He walked away fast as if he was running away from her.

Change? How could she change? Mythili saw him getting into his car and driving away. He did not look back even once. Her heart was pounding. 'Go to his house.' All she could think of was to meet Akash again. She also wanted to see his baby boy. She checked herself, 'She did not even see the baby and already she started loving him.' Her instinct told her meeting Akash was like playing with fire and she would be hurt again, if not more. The next two days, she fought with the idea of meeting Akash again.

But like a bug attracted to the flaming candle, Mythili could not stop herself from meeting Akash. She did not expect anything from Akash, at least she thought so. But somewhere in the corner of her heart, she felt she had hope and she did not even know about it.

✧

AFTER A FEW days, Mythili stood looking at Akash's house. When they first met, he showed the house to her proudly, "That's my house." It was a duplex house with a drive in to the main door and also a parking spot. There were lots of exotic flower plants and the plants were arranged in a way that the flowers made either a contrast or a perfect match. As she looked up, she saw Akash carrying the baby on his shoulder. He seemed to tenderly hug the baby and Mythili's heart burst out for both of them. She hurried to the watchman and told him who she was and that Akash would be expecting her. The watchman allowed her inside and made her sit in the guest room and went up to tell him.

As Mythili saw the wall covered with pictures of Nisha, she had mixed feelings about her. Though she knew it was Akash who was guilty, she loved him so much that she believed that Nisha was the reason for their break-up. And yet dying at such a young age, she felt sorry for her. She looked at her charming face and brilliant eyes. And suddenly she was jealous of her. She was transferred back to the day when Akash broke up with her. She could not stop him. She was heartbroken that day. She wanted to hurt him by going to Nisha and telling her all about their affair and that it continued even after they were engaged. But she loved Akash so much that she could not hurt him. Hurting him would not bring him back to her. She cried for weeks together, lying down in the empty apartment as empty as her heart, not moving for she felt so numb that she doubted her existence. What was she doing here? She rose out of the chair to get away before it was too late when she heard the sweet voice.

"Hello Mythili." Akash seemed pleased that she came.

As if in hypnosis, Mythili forgot everything she thought a second ago and she turned to face him, "Hello. I hope I am not intruding."

"Oh! No. I am glad that you have come." Looking at Mythili, he felt fresh, as if nothing has happened these past two years. She made him feel young. Looking at her eyes, he was surprised she was still in love with him.

"I just could not resist seeing your son." Mythili was surprised when she knew just at that moment she was not lying. She really wanted to see the baby.

"Oh! Then you are not here to see me. You are here only to see the cutest guy in town. Time is so cruel, I have already become old." He did a fake sigh, which made Mythili laugh.

"Yes, so now can I meet the cute one?" she still could not stop smiling.

"Please do come in. He actually has just gone to sleep, but I will take you to the nursery and you can see him." Akash showed her the way.

Mythili was slightly surprised at his formality. Even when they first met, he was never formal, "You are being too formal. I guess you have changed a bit." She looked deeply into his eyes, searching desperately to see a hint of love for her.

His face turned grave, "I had to change." He looked away from her intense eyes.

They went into the nursery; Mythili thought it was the most beautiful room in the house. Everything in the room was filled with shades of violet or lavender. "Did Nisha love violets?" Mythili blurted out and then caught her tongue.

"Not really, it's just that she did not like conventions. For nurseries, the architect suggested that if it was a girl, pink was the colour and if it was a boy, blue was the colour. She could not wait till the baby was born and then started the arrangements too. She was a perfect planner; she wanted everything perfect for the baby. So she chose a neutral color for the room. Isn't it lovely? Every time I see the room, it takes my breath away. You can say that she did the whole interior designing for this room. The interior designer was frustrated by the time it was over. He was just an information tool for her and she got the best out of him." Akash was again lost in his own thoughts.

Mythili's heart sank, 'He is deeply in love with her.' She knew Akash was transformed back in time, where at the same place Nisha worked busily with her very pregnant belly, bossing everyone about the arrangements. But she could not understand why she was being so upset about all this. Suddenly she emerged out of her thoughts when Akash called her to see the baby.

"What do you know? He is awake. The little fellow knows the scent of a beautiful woman." Akash put a finger in his little palm and played with him.

Mythili's heart skipped, Akash so smoothly said such things and would not even know that they work like charms mesmerizing her to fall in love with him each time he talked. She took hold of herself and went forward to see the baby. The baby was looking at his father and laughing when he was making funny faces and when he saw another person leaning over to see him, he looked at her with a puzzle on his face as if asking who she was? Mythili could not believe how beautiful the baby was. His questioning expression, his liveliness, and when she saw his eyes, she was spellbound. She touched his cheek delicately as if he would get hurt if she was not careful. The baby, not knowing who the stranger was, looked at her with a doubtful face. Mythili started making funny faces herself. Seeing that even the stranger was funny, the baby laughed and his eyes shone. Mythili could not resist, "He will be even more handsome than you when he grows up." And she stopped; she should not have said that.

"Well thanks. So you still think this old man is handsome, do you?" Laughed Akash.

"Err…it's just a metaphor. Don't flatter yourself." Mythili defended herself with a smile. Then she looked at the baby, he yawned and she wanted to take him in her arms. "Can I hold him?"

"Sure. He is all yours. I will be glad to give him to you. He cries all night and day; he wants milk all the time. That's all. He is not much trouble." He smiled.

Mythili slowly put her hand under the baby's head to support him and lifted him slowly and put him on her left shoulder and involuntarily moved as if she was the baby's cradle. Then she went and sat at an easy chair that was just by the wooden cradle's side.

She tapped the baby's back softly placing her left cheek on the baby's head.

Akash watched in amazement how smoothly the baby drifted to sleep and calmly sat by her side on a small sofa stool. In a hushed tone he spoke, "That was amazing Mythili. I remember now, you must have your experience from those naughty nephew and niece of yours. How are they?"

Mythili frowned; when her sister knew about her love affair with Akash, she asked her to leave the house or marry a person she thought fit for her. But she could not do that, so she was now staying in the hostel. She shushed him and slowly placed the baby in the cradle and kissed him on the cheek. Akash looked thankful that the baby was sleeping.

Both of them came out of the nursery and went back to the drawing room. Akash sank into the sofa very tired. Mythili sat by his side. She did not say a word. She wanted him to speak out.

After a moment of silence, that long heart-wrenching moment, Akash spoke, "She wanted everything so perfect. She was such a hard worker that she pushed herself beyond limits. Even though she was eight months pregnant, she used to poke her nose into every single minute detail. Panting and supporting the back with her hand on her hips, she would move around just the way she did while she worked in the office. I did not stop her, Mythili. I was burdened with work in the office as Nisha had stopped coming to office from the seventh month onwards. I knew she was exerting herself…" Akash paused.

Mythili placed her hand hesitantly over his shoulder; she felt the pain Akash was feeling. For the first time she saw Akash crying. She tried to wipe the tears off, seeing his tears made her eyes wet. Akash spoke in a very desperate voice, "I always thought that tears tell you the intensity of pain inside you, but no. They say nothing. I heard someone say, tears relieve your pain, but it is all crap. No matter how much you cry, nothing changes. Nothing! She nearly completed the term, there was just ten days left and then one day she shouted at a carpenter for doing things wrong with a silly shelf by the chair's side, something about not being the adequate height to put the story book down and suddenly her BP raised so much that she had to be taken to the emergency room immediately. I was there at home. When we took her to the doctor, he said she was having labour pains and the next one hour was the most horrible one hour of my life...the doctor tells me my wife is dead. Imagine that! She was just fine about two hours ago, very happy and now she is no more. I thought I will go mad; I was crying without any sense and the nurse asks me to calm down for I have a baby boy to take care of. Life does not make any sense Mythili, but I have to live for this boy. I loved him instantly. He just looked at me, even though the light hurt his little eyes, and from that day I knew what love really was. But when I saw Nisha lying in the bed, lifeless......" Akash faltered as his voice was shaking, he started crying deeply as if he had lost something inside him.

Mythili did not know what to do. She moved a little closer to him, gripped his shoulder to calm him down and suddenly Akash hugged and started crying loudly, "I don't know what to do...I don't know what to do! How will I take care of the business? How will I take care of my baby? She left me all alone. What can I do? The pain inside me grows everyday, it feels as if living is becoming a burden everyday. I don't know what to do?"

Mythili hugged him and listened to him, "Don't worry. Trust yourself. You can do it. I will be there for you. I will help you take care of the baby. Don't worry Akash. Be brave."

Akash hugged her more tightly, "You will be there for me? Thank you so much. I think all this is happening to me because I broke your heart." Mythili had tears in her eyes, but she did not stop consoling him. Akash went on, "But such a big punishment for such a small mistake? You tell me Mythili, is it fair......" Akash released her from his embrace and looked at Mythili, she had tears in her eyes too, and she looked down.

"Mythili don't cry; I really hurt you, didn't I? Please forgive me." He caught her hands and asked for her forgiveness profusely.

Mythili felt embarrassed, "No need to apologise. Lot of things have happened since then. Don't add up to your baggage of loss. I never hated you Akash." She looked into the troubled eyes of Akash. She saw a different shade in them. His tears stopped and he looked at her for some kind of comfort. He just sat there with a hazy look. Mythili stood up, "Come take my hand, I think it is best you take rest for now." She looked around for the bedroom. She saw one just beside the nursery. She forced Akash to get up and took him to the bed and made him lie down. "Lie down here for sometime and don't think of anything. I will prepare some tea for you. It will relax you." He nodded, just like her nephew does so many times. She searched for the kitchen, which was very orderly and after a few minutes returned with some hot tea in her hand. Akash looked better now.

"Have this tea and sleep for some time. I will be here till you wake up," she gave the tea cup to Akash. Akash smiled and sat up on the bed. He took the tea cup and put it on the table beside it. He looked at her and caught her shoulders. He came closer to her. Mythili did not understand what was happening – she had not wanted to.

She closed her eyes. No fear or thought crossed her mind. She felt his lips on hers. He kissed her slowly on her lower lip, paused and then kissed at the same spot. She felt alive, heart pulsing like never before, yearning for more. She was in a space where gravity had never worked before. She forgot who she was. All she wanted was to have her empty heart replaced by another heart. She wanted no existence of her own. She only wanted Akash. She wanted to become one with him. If it was possible for two souls to become one and burn together, she wanted it. Nothing, let be it time – the heartless cold time, should separate them, for she had endured a hopeless part of her life without love and life miserably acknowledged that she could not love anyone else. She could not even love herself without his love. Time stood still. She didn't care if it was a dream or a fantasy, she would rather be called mad and lost in it than come to the reality of life. She just waited, quivering like a lifeless plant for Akash to pour life into her. She felt his lips on hers and she opened her eyes and kissed him back.

Akash felt feverish. There was always something irresistible in Mythili. She looked like a fawn wanting to be fondled. He felt happy to see her in his home. Her tender care made her enticing and made him secure. She held herself with grace even though he hurt her. He just wanted to forget everything and hug her and kiss her. She kissed him back and he just grabbed her closer.

Like lovers that newly found their love, they kissed and caressed each other. Their passions leapt with rage and fire in their hearts, each trying to find what they wanted. A kiss sent them back to a time of utopia. They found their way back to that night shining in the glitters of the crackers and rockets that burst into a fountain of colours. Their hearts burst brighter than the colours that night. Their bodies felt an ecstasy unknown to them. They caressed cheek to cheek, lip to lip, and skin to skin. They knew not but to quench their thirst for love.

As she lay enclosed under his body, an untimely cry made them aware of someone there. Their lips parted and the skin went cold. Akash got off the bed and ran towards the cry, leaving a parching soul behind. Akash took the baby into his arm and started cradling him and asked the baby what he wanted. He waited for an answer and the baby cried on. He felt the diaper wet and changed it. The baby instantly stopped crying and looked at his father, sucking his thumb. He felt warm lying on his father's bare chest and smiled at him. Akash looked at his son, "You know my son…your father is a fool!"

As he dozed off into dreams of speechless dreams, Akash left him and came into the bedroom to face his folly yet again. He looked at her just completing her make up. She looked uncertain and helpless. This angered Akash, "Why do you look helpless all the time? What is the meaning of this? You come into my home, play with my kid, and try to seduce a man who just lost his wife! Have you no sense as to behave accordingly? You think this is a chance to come back into my life. You think by alluring me, you will get me. Don't you understand? I have a baby now to look after. I cannot fool around with you now. I have to think what is best for him. It's just been three months since her death, I can't think of a partner right now." Mythili was shocked.

Akash continued, "Why do you look shocked? Life is like that. You don't act with your mind; you act with your heart. Do you think I will appreciate whatever has happened today? Do you think I will marry you? NEVER! I love Nisha. She was a strong person. She always acted what her mind told her. She controlled her emotions. I love that. Do you understand why I left you?" He shouted at Mythili with anger. Mythili burst out into silent tears. That calmed down Akash. He shrank into the sofa by the door of the bedroom. "Please go away. I am sorry."

"Give me a second." Mythili went into the bathroom adjoining the bedroom and locked herself inside. Her mind was reeling. What was happening? The words he so harshly said were ringing in her ears. She did not understand who she kissed right now. The person who was shouting at her right now was not the person she fell in love with. 'DO YOU THINK I WILL MARRY YOU? NEVER!' She heard his voice speaking those words harsher and harsher. She felt panicky. Her hope along with her heart broke into a million pieces. She felt her life drain away with her happiness. How was she to live now? She did not feel the air around her. She breathed shallow. She staggered to find the tap and put some cold water on her face. She tried to calm herself. She wiped herself and opened the door.

Akash was still sitting in the same position with his head bent down and his two hands on his head, with elbows on his legs. She walked past him in silence and looked back. She lost her voice even to say bye. He did not move. As she was about to go away, she heard a voice. She went in to look at the baby. The baby was sucking the honey sucker that was given by his father. She bent to kiss the baby goodbye and the baby caught her chain. Mythili was overwhelmed. Akash once gifted the chain to her and when the baby caught it, she lifted the baby and held him close to her chest and strangely she felt happy. She was relieved that she could love someone other than Akash. She tried to keep the baby back in the crib, and removed the chain from the baby's grip. She could not. She wanted to be with the baby. She had no hope of Akash's love and she treated her so cruelly.

'I can have this baby's love at least and I will teach him how to treat women.' She did not think anymore further. She looked back and saw Akash still sitting with his hands on his head. She lifted the baby, put a blanket on him, and softly walked beyond the bedroom door, and watched out for the watchman; he was filling up water in the water tank that was underground. She slowly walked down the garden and got to the big iron gate.

As she passed out of the gate, the watchman called her, "Madam, should I call an auto?"

Standing such a way that the watchman would not see the baby, she arched back, "No. I will go by bus."

"Ok Madam, good day!" Bowed the watchman.

"Good day indeed." She hurried past a few houses there and found an auto to her hostel.

December 2006

SHE LAUGHED AT herself. All her life she had tried to catch Akash and now she was running away from him. She had long feared this day and yet she always thought it was in the distant future. That day stealing his son saved her life. She never imagined being alive if it weren't for Bittu. She would have been so depressed that she would have killed herself. At that moment when she took the baby away from his house, she wondered if she did it to take revenge on him, but later she justified herself, *'He destroyed my life and I have taken away his.'*

Since the day she got Bittu, she never turned back. She had not cried or felt sorry for herself. She never wished she might have done things in a different way. She worked hard and provided everything Akash could have given him. Every day she feared what would have happened if Akash found out where she lived. She was sure that when he will find her, he would kill her at that instant. The clock struck the sixth time and then she remembered she had to pick up Bittu from the picnic bus. She drove her Tata Indica to the school, where Bittu was waiting impatiently. Only few of them were left. When he saw his mother come, he ran to her and got into the car's front side, which was opened and sat beside the driver's seat.

Mythili looked at him crossed, "Where are kids supposed to sit Bittu?"

"It's only for today Mom. I want to tell you about my picnic." But guessing his Mom would not allow it no matter what, he got out and sat in the back seat with a sulking face. Mythili laughed and put the seat belt on him. "I have prepared a wonderful dinner for you. You can tell me all about Moni..sh then."

"Mooom!" Bittu looked appalled.

Mythili laughed and drove towards home. Bittu was very excited to go out with just his friends for the first time. He was telling her about the games they had played and how noisy the girls were. Mythili was completely lost in the conversation as she parked the car and they let themselves into the house that she did not notice the dark figure standing in between the trees looking at them. The mar looked sick, but now he seemed to have revived.

Mythili arranged his favourite food of *aloo parathas* and *paneer butter masala*, a glass of lassi by his side, to which he held his nostrils together. Bittu did not like curd or *lassi*. Mythili smiled because even Akash hated *lassi*. But Mythili generally forced him to drink it after his dinner. So Bittu put a piece of *paneer* aside, so that when he finished drinking the lassi, he would eat the *paneer* piece and did not have that unpleasant taste in his mouth. She thought Bittu was a genius when she first saw his little 'taste' technique.

✧

ON THAT FULL moon day, when the moon stood out in the sky reigning the night, a green-eyed man stood looking through the window at the little boy and thanked God with a smile on his face. He took out something out from his pocket, it shone in the moonlight. He put it back in his pocket. He looked at his watch, it was nine o'clock and he waited for the kid to sleep. The kid was already feeling sleepy. He watched him go to sleep. He wanted to wait till 9:30 to make sure the kid slept.

He had gone half-mad the day when he found his son was missing. He called up the watchman to ask if anyone had come in and he said no. It took a while for him to realise that Mythili might have taken him. He did not know where she lived. He went to her sister's house, then to the hostel, but she was not there. She had no relatives that she could go to or any close friends. He did not understand why she might have taken him. Did she kidnap him for money? She was not that kind of a girl. But he didn't know her anymore. He had put up posters, given ads in newspapers and TV for almost a year and then he understood that she must have gone out of the city. He took the help of the police and checked her account, it had zero balance. He was totally lost. He was no longer looking after his father's or his in-laws' business. His father and Nisha's father looked after it. He could not explain anything to them, why Mythili had kidnapped the baby and even after one year why there were no ransom threats. He no longer felt guilty for what he had done to Mythili. He hated her. He hired a private investigator. He also could not do much, because Mythili was cut off from any social contact for the past one year and she had a fight with her friend just a few days before the kidnap. The 'friend' also did not know what happened. A few girls in the hostel told them that she came in a hurry and left with her suitcase. In the hostel, they always keep things in a suitcase and lock, so it just took a little time for her to pack and go. No one knew she actually left.

He had lost all hope until a week ago. One day, Mrs. Sharma who was a new acquaintance of his mother, came to their house.

In the living room there was a hanging of Akash's close-up. She looked at the photo and was amazed at how closely the boy she saw in Horsley Hills resembled Akash. She obviously did not know the kidnapping. Mrs. Choudary asked her how old the boy was. Mrs. Sharma, who did not understand why Mrs. Choudary was so anxious, answered her "It was his sixth birthday." Mrs. Choudary was overjoyed and thought that finally her prayers have been answered. She asked her to tell where and when she saw the boy. Mrs. Sharma told her that she took a trip to the new and modified Horsley Hills that early summer around March. She loved the hotel that she stayed there. One day while she was having dinner at the hotel's buffet section, she saw a little birthday party. A lady who looked like the mother of the boy was celebrating the boy's birthday with a few staff members. She could not forget the party because the mother looked very lovely, she was a yoga instructor after all and that the boy's eyes were stunning green. To Mrs. Sharma's amazement, Mrs. Choudary thanked her profusely and hurried off to tell Akash. He rushed to Horsley Hills. But he could not approach her just like that. She can do anything and she might even harm his Abhinav. Nisha thought of the name 'Abhinav' for the kid, so though he had no chance to name his son, he remembered his son with that name.

After reaching Horsley Hills, he watched Mythili's every move and he saw Abhinav for the first time all dressed in a school dress to go to school. He could not hold himself back. The last time he saw his son was when he hardly was able to crawl and now he is running wildly. He wanted to approach him and hug him. But he was scared. Mythili looked after him well. He did not know what she wanted to do with him. He was still puzzled by her rash decision. He would have never thought of her as an impulsive woman. She was always so patient with everyone! He observed for one week and then he decided that it was the best time to approach Mythili.

He had played this moment in his mind a million times. Every time the same scene appeared. When he found Mythili, he would take his son away from her and would kill her. He hated HER that much.

Mythili was now in the kitchen, washing dishes. He slowly crept up to the front door and made sure no one was looking. He pressed the doorbell. He heard Mythili screw the tap shut. He waited for her to open the door. He heard the doorknob open and he stood close to the door. Mythili opened the door and looked up, shocked. Akash put his hand on her mouth and shoved her inside. Mythili did not fight. She just stood looking at him. Akash locked the door. He looked towards the boy's room and looked around. He took her to her bedroom, slapped her hard, and pushed her on the bed. He locked the door.

Mythili just kept staring at him. She could not think. Akash turned to face her and took out a gun pointing to her face. Silence resounded back. Mythili had feared this moment, but now, she was not scared to see him. "Please put the gun away. There is no need for this," Mythili spoke boldly; she was surprised at her own poise.

But Akash was irritated, "No need for this? What do you mean no need for this? You steal my son, disappear for six years, you tried to ruin my life, and should I be calm?" Akash held out the gun, his hand trembling, but he gripped it tight. "Why did you do this to me Mythili? Do I deserve this punishment that you have given me? Why did you take him away? I don't understand." Akash's bloodshot eyes questioned her pleadingly.

"You don't even know why I took away your son?" Mythili shrugged her head. Akash blinked innocently. "You destroyed my life! You made me fall in love with you. You showed me what love is and you took it away with a snap."

Akash was disgusted, "YOU are accusing me? Before my marriage whatever happened was a mistake. I had to make a choice.

I was really sorry for that. If you had gone on with your life just as I did, you would have been happy."

"Happy! Not everyone falls in love twice Akash. You knew about my life, you knew how hard it was for me then to just get on with daily life. You come and save me, and then you just drop me, lie to me, and go and marry another girl. How can I get on with my life? I was madly in love with you!" Mythili's heart was bursting out. She did not care about the gun anymore.

"Love! If you had such problem getting on with your life, I never saw it when I was getting married or the year after it. You did not do anything at that time, then why did you take away my son when I needed him the most?"

"I am ashamed that I ever fell in love with you Akash. You have no clue of what I had endured from you. The day I came to your home, all I wanted was to see you and your son. Then you kiss me. I was no better from the time you left me that day, it took all my strength to go on with my life and then you kiss me and I fell in love with you all over again. Can't you understand such a simple fact? And suddenly you remember you have responsibility and you insult me…" Mythili could not breathe. She gulped with pain.

Akash was more irritated than ever, "Mythili, you made a choice that you could not handle. I never promised you anything."

"Promise! You are talking about promises? When you kiss me that was an unsaid promise." Mythili retorted back.

"What kind of a world do you live in? A kiss is a promise? I have never heard such a concept before." Akash smirked.

"Hoo! Don't be so cruel Akash." Mythili could not bear Akash talking that way.

"CRUEL? Who was being cruel all these years? After I see my son I don't even know if he will accept me. Why were YOU so cruel to me? When you took him away, my wife died just a few months ago…did you ever think I could have survived?" Akash could not hold the gun any longer. He put his hand down still holding the gun. Mythili was silently looking at the gun.

"I took him away because…" Mythili paused as Akash looked at her unconvinced, "I didn't want him to grow up like you." Mythili spoke silently closing her eyes.

"Like me?" Akash could not believe his ears.

"Yes. You cheat a girl and you don't even feel sorry. You think a simple sorry would all make it up. You believe if there is no verbal acknowledgement, there is no promise made. No matter what way you twist them Akash, you have cheated me. You did it not once but twice. The boy is motherless, so I took him away." Mythili spoke decidedly.

"And you want him to be like you? How ironic!" Akash questioned her.

Just then there was a soft knock on the door. "Mama…are you there? I heard some man talking."

Akash froze. He put the gun again in his pocket and waved his hand to open the door. Mythili sighed that now it was time that Bittu would leave her. She opened the door and Bittu stood there rubbing his eyes with his right hand and dragging a teddy bear with the other hand. Mythili hugged Bittu and kissed his cheek and forehead. Tears would not stop coming. Bittu looked at her mother crying, "Why are you crying mama? Who is that man? Has he said anything to you?" He tried to look at Akash more closely, who was standing in a shadowy place.

Akash was not sure what to do. He was sure that he would kill her when he found her out, but some of the things she spoke made him feel guilty that he unknowingly was the reason for his own sorrow. His hate for her has faded since he saw her with Abhinav; she took care of his son comfortably. He saw her hug his son and something gripped his heart seeing his son love her back just the same. If anything happened to her, he would get hurt too. His mind was exploding with all the memories of pain and despair when the little angelic voice called him, "Daddy! You came back daddy."

Akash felt his heart beat faster and he kneeled down to hug 'his' son who was now running towards him. Bittu wrapped his hands around his neck and slowly kissed his cheek. Akash could not believe how sweet scented his son was and his soft little lips kissing him had made all the pain vanish away. Akash hugged him tenderly, "Bittu, I missed you a lot."

To this Bittu was surprised, "Daddy! Call me Abhinav, I like it better. My friends tease me when mom calls me Bittu. They will tease me double when they hear you also call me by the same name." He did not notice his father's eyes filled with tears hiding his surprise. He looked at Mythili questioningly.

Mythili was also sniffing with glistening eyes. She gave a gesture to wait. She remembered the day when she was picking up Bittu; she saw a lilac blanket by his side that was hand knitted Abhinav with golden thread. She took it along with Bittu.

But Akash did not care how Bittu knew him to be his father or how Mythili knew the name Abhinav. All he wanted was to hold Abhinav closely to his ailing heart. He felt his hate melt away, he no longer felt sad, Bittu had softened his heart just in those few minutes. Akash sat in a rocking chair by the side of the bed and Bittu lay on his father, talking to him about all the things that came into his mind and suddenly he became serious, "Daddy, just wait. I will show you something." He ran away to his room. Akash took a deep breath and looked at anxious Mythili's face. He was about to ask something when he heard Bittu running back. Akash recognised the lilac hand knitted blanket in Bittu's hand that Nisha had made for Bittu. Then he knew how Mythili had named him Abhinav. He was confused, even more so, when Bittu showed the wedding photograph of him and Nisha.

Bittu gave the blanket to Akash, "See Daddy I still have mom's blanket with me. I have not soiled it. *Amma* is always with me if I keep it carefully." Akash took the blanket in his hand and touched the golden letters. He closed his eyes 'Nisha.'

"Daddy I talk to *Amma* daily every night and I tell her about my school. Now we can both talk to her daily Daddy, so she won't miss us. Mama said God will take good care of *Amma* and that she is an angel and would always look after us both. It is Mama's and my secret that *Amma* is an angel. Now it is *our* secret." Bittu whispered at the last sentence. Akash hugged him tightly and tears burst out. He looked at Mythili and he no longer hated her. Bittu knew who his parents were and that's all that mattered right now.

Bittu fell asleep on him and even though Akash did not want to let go off him, he took Bittu to bed. He pulled the door close and came back to the drawing room, where Mythili sat brooding gloomily. He sat, drawing a chair opposite to her. The fridge made that peculiar noise 'zmmmm' that people have become so accustomed to and the tube light flickered invisibly on both of them. Neither could speak.

Finally Mythili gave in, "Akash, I am sorry, very sorry. But I still want to be part of his life. I love him as if he was my own son. Please do not hate me so much that you banish me. I cannot live without seeing him and..." Mythili stopped as she saw the hate flickering in his eyes again. She put her sari *pallu* over her mouth and wept mutely.

Akash was still holding the lilac blanket. He looked up and asked her, "You told Bittu that Nisha was his *Amma* and that I was his father. Who did you say 'you' were? What did you tell him about the reason of my absence?"

"I told him that I was a common friend of you both and that his mother died after a few days after his birth. I told him that you had to go to a place very far to do an important thing that would take a lot of time. I told him that I would take care of him as his mother. So he calls me Mama and he calls Nisha *Amma*. I could not lie to him about his mother and father. I wanted him to know who they were and I knew someday, either you would find me or I would bring Bittu to you, so I showed him the wedding picture that I took from your bedroom that day. I took it to remind me of how much you hurt me lest I would fall in love with you again."

She spoke those words as if she believed them, but Akash could see she loved him even now. Akash smiled sarcastically. He took a deep breath, "I hate you Mythili. I do not deserve what you have done to me." Mythili started to argue, but Akash did not stop, "But I realise I hurt you a lot so I have decided not to send you to jail. I will take Bittu away. He is still small and will slowly forget you. You are never to come near my house or Bittu. If you do," Akash spoke firmly, "I will send you to jail that instant." Akash rose and went into Bittu's room to sit by his side, waiting for the first ray of light, bringing with it hope.

Mythili locked herself in the bedroom. She cried and cried, wishing her heart would stop beating just for a moment. In trying to save herself, she had put herself in another heartbreaking situation. She did not know what she would do now. Then suddenly she became aware that she felt better! She no longer felt the guilt that was haunting her for so long that her heart always felt heavy. She knew then she was going to survive a life without Bittu, her sweet Bittu.

✧

THE NEXT MORNING, she said goodbye to Bittu who was very happy and very brave. Akash asked her to lie to Bittu that she would come to their home in a few days. But Mythili knew they would never meet again, it was just a matter of time. She kissed him goodbye.

She noted the date down in her diary and wrote down, '*When you love someone so much that you fear losing them, there is just a fine line between love and selfishness. I crossed it once. Now I know what true love means. I will miss Bittu terribly, but I know being with his father was the only place for him. I had to let go off him to love him!*'

❂

3

Peetam

The Accident

IT WAS A sunny afternoon in the middle of April when the mercury was rising, and dry wind prowled through the empty playground that made even the green leaves droop in contempt. The sun-baked ground and the hot air together created mirages, but here in Hyderabad, people knew not to trust a mirage. The iron swings and mini merry-go-rounds seemed to melt in that hot summer afternoon. No one would venture out at that time; but then a boy, a 13-year-old boy sat by the side of the swing, kneeling, with his face turned away, looking at something very intently. No one knew how long he had been sitting that way, but the atmosphere around him felt sinister. There was no doubt that whatever he was looking at, he found it from the sand that was in the playing ground; as it was dug out quite a bit.

Just outside the main gate, a couple was searching for someone. They could not see the boy anywhere in their sight. They went into the watchman's shed. The watchman was sleeping on a wooden chair with his legs on a large stone, and a towel on his head and eyes to beat the heat. They woke him up to ask him if he had seen their boy. Scorning at them, the watchman woke up, wiping his face with the towel and came out and looked around. For a common eye, the boy in the playground would have been concealed, but the watchman knew every part of the ground. He told them that the boy was near the swing and pointed him to his parents with his guarding stick in the left hand, ferociously scratching his head with the right hand. The parents first did not see the boy, but then finally saw him. The mother was about to run towards him when the father stopped and showed her the scorching sun, so they got into the car and drove it into the play zone. The car stopped just by the boy's right side and his mother saw him holding something, and it shone in the sun. The mother knew instantly what it was; she panicked, and shouted at the boy to throw it away. The father was confused about why his wife was shouting and turned to see the boy. Then, both the father and the mother were frightened when the boy turned and scowled at them. The mother recouped and as she was about to get down from the car, the car seemed to move. The mother looked angrily at the father, "Gautam! Why did u start the ca....." and her voice trailed away in horror. Gautam was not even touching the wheel of the car or the accelerator, but the accelerator was pushed so hard that the car whirled violently and crashed into the tree ahead of them, before any of the passengers in the car knew what had happened.

The loud noise startled the boy as if he woke from a deep sleep. He slowly walked towards the car and saw blood splattered on the broken glass. He sat calmly on a bench watching the blood drip from the car. The watchman, who came running after hearing the crash, saw the kid sitting near the car looking at his parents. As he came nearer, he saw petrol leaking out from the car and he grabbed the boy to take him to a safer place. Just when they reached a good distance from the car, the car exploded into flames and both of them sat down where they were watching the car burn in flames. The acidic smell of smoke filled their lungs. The watchman looked at the boy to see if he had any bruises; when he had made sure he had none, he looked at the boy's eyes and was scared. They were blank.....they showed no fear or hurt. 'The boy had just seen his parents die and he has no feelings!' he thought; but pushed the thought away, 'May be he is in shock.'

As the people outside the school came running in and some people ran to STD booths calling the Fire Station, the boy remained with the watchman, watching the angry flames. The flames seemed to dance in rage and he heard them calling his name "ISHWAK.... COME.....ISHWAK."

Tulasimandiram

ONLY TULASI, THE holy herb signifying purity and known for its healing powers, could be compared to the house of Pandit Vishwanath. The house was no less than a temple in its environment and austerity and hence the name, Tulasimandiram (the abode of Tulasi). The house was presented to Pandit Vishwanath's grandfather Pandit Siva Rama Krishna, by the generous Zamindar of his era, who believed that scholars and artists should be honoured and taken care of. Even now after nearly fifty years, Tulasimandiram did not age a day old and looked magnificent in the humble village of Panipakam.

One could see Tulasimandiram embedded in between a tropical garden of flowers in the front yard, and a thick green patch of trees in the backyard. The whole house had a brick wall perimeter and the gate of the front yard was made of wood and it had Lord Ganesha carved on it. The gate opened to a rocky path, which had worn out smoothly over the years, giving it a riverbed look; people who walked that path would often wonder how good it must feel to walk barefoot. On either side of the paths, there were flowering plants like Jasmine, Chrysanthemums, Lilies, Marigold, Hibiscus, Rose, and Kanakambarams (the orange half flowers). The roses were the local ones that had the delicious Rose scent mesmerizing the senses; albeit the hybrid roses looked more aesthetic. But Parvathi, Pandit's wife, preferred the local roses to hybrids. There were logs arranged in the fashion of picnic benches and chairs in the middle of the garden. As the path was about to end, it divided into two, running sideways from the Holy Tulasi plant that was planted in a classic Tulasi bearing mud pot that had a triangular engraving in it, where a oil lamp could be lighted which the devotees offered as a part of their daily prayers.

Every morning Parvathi offered her prayers there and lighted the incense which lingered in the air there and relaxed the senses. The divided paths ended in two steps that rise to the platform of the lobby. The lobby was nothing but four wooden poles supporting a steel mesh that was totally covered with little pink-flowered creepers, making the steel mesh a cool roof. The sun could not penetrate such perfect sunscreen and even in hot summers, the family could sit in the lobby for hours.

The lobby opened into the house, and the main door was made of heavy rosewood with classic Indian carvings on it. Very few houses these days had such doors and the door itself was an exquisite art piece with the borders of flowery creepers, mango-shaped motifs, classic lotus petal carvings, and little brass bells that made a 'ting' every time one bumped into it. Years of use and the good quality of the rosewood had made it look shinier, mostly on the places where people tend to touch it more. Like the gates of heaven, the great rosewood door opened into a small passageway that ended the path, divided into the left and right corridors that again joined on the other side, forming a square-shaped cement platform which descended into the earth by two steps in the heart of the house leading to the 'Peetam.' To a common eye, the Peetam was not an out-of-ordinary place; it was just a raised platform of earth in the middle of the house that had been decorated by *kumkuma* and *pasupu* (the holy powders of red kumkum and turmeric), but it was a great sacred place which only few people knew.

The Peetam was actually surrounded by the house. The elevated cement platform led into the different rooms of Poojamandiram (place to worship the God); on the right side corner at the end of labyrinth, the room was on the east side of the house. This room was the most cleaned part of the house, it sparkled in every corner. The upper side of the door had a garland of tender green mango leaves tied up in a row, making the room more sacred and aesthetic in a simple way. The great Pandit Vishwanath spent most of his time in this room meditating and no one dared to disturb him in the house. He was an ardent worshipper of Goddess Durga and at any given time of the day, the incense poured out of the room along with the Vedic chants of Pandit Vishwanath's heavenly voice. An oil lamp always burnt before the Goddess, even through the night, as a symbol of uninterrupted devotion of the family towards Goddess Durga. There was always an evergreen supply of flowers and fruits from the garden which was maintained excellently by his wife Parvathi and their eldest son Parusuram, who was in all terms, an obedient son of Vishwanath and Parvathi.

The storeroom stood next to the worshipping room. The whole year's rice, cereals, pulses, and other necessary things were placed in that room. All the things needed for worship were also placed there. The storeroom was on the corner on the east side of the house; next to it on the north side of the house were the rooms of Vishwanath's two sons. The first son, Parusuram was married ten years ago, had three sons, but the wife died due to a grave illness. The second son, Achyuta, was married to Kavita and they had only one daughter, Gita (named after the holy Hindu book). They lived in the room next to Parusuram's. The north side ended there and on the west side of the house, was the kitchen and attached to it was the dining room (traditional). The kitchen was huge, as often many functions were performed in the house, where a number of people were invited for lunch and Parvathi would just smile and cook even for 100 people. Both her daughters-in-law would also help her in such events and there was a kind of traditional discipline in them about doing the work, even though both the young women preferred not to take so much of burden. Adjoining the kitchen, there was the dining room, where all of the men sat first and were served by the Lady of the house and the daughters-in-law. The sons preferred eating in the steel plates, but Pandit Vishwanath always dined in the banana leaves. They were more hygienic and recyclable, he always said. After the men had eaten, the women would eat the food and the youngest son would often serve the ladies, as he thought it was only appropriate. That is the way things are even till now in almost all parts of India.

The kitchen opened into the backyard, the most beautiful backyard one could ever see; that was fully equipped from spicy and healing shrubs to fruity trees. The backyard started with shrubs filled with curry leaves plants, coriander, and mint which was mixed with vegetable plants like lady's finger, brinjal, bitter gourd, and beans etc. There was a path of stones, not a continuous one but single soft cornered stones placed a feet away from each other, the grass grew around the stones and the path. Parvathi was very proud of her garden. She had put in all her heart into the garden, which in return gave her joy of living every day.

On the south side of the house were two more rooms, and in one lived the youngest son, Deependra. He was married to Shanti, and they had a son, Aditya. The room next to theirs was always shut except when a guest came home. No one dared venture in to the room, if they did, they would see the wrath of their grandfather.

Coming back to the west side of the house, there was a big room for Pandit Vishwanath and Parvathi, and beside it was the smaller room where all the kids, the three sons of Parúsuram, Phani, Siddharth, and Vikas; Gita, the daughter of Achyuta; and Aditya, the son of Deependra slept. All the kids were in the age group of ten-fifteen, the eldest being Phani and the youngest being Aditya. Gita was only 12 years of age, but she was a protégée of Pandit Vishwanath, she was well versed in the Vedas. Everyone in the village was astonished when they heard her chanting. Anyone who heard her would just stand mesmerised. People in the village felt that she is Goddess *Saraswathi* (goddess of knowledge) personified; the avatar of *Saraswathi*. One could swear to see a pinch of jealousy in Pandit Vishwanath's sons' eyes, none of whom possessed such a talent as the twelve year old.

That fateful day, when somewhere in the city, where a car struck a tree before a blank-faced boy in an empty school playground, a telegram would change the life of a simple, happy family, whose life revolved around devotion and discipline of the Vedas. The postman of the village slowed down his rambling cycle before

Tulasimandiram. He enjoyed coming to the home of the great Pandit, and especially looked forward for the buttermilk that the lady of the house gave him; Parvathi had magic in her cooking. But he had never brought a telegram to this house before. He mumbled, 'A telegram never brings good news,' his experience told him. The postman with a letter is always appreciated than the postman with a telegram. As he entered the path, he bowed before the holy Tulasi plant with devotion and he entered the lobby, he could see no one outside, but could hear little Gita chanting the Vedas again. He stood outside listening to the delightful voice, when Parusuram came out and saw him.

"*Namaskaram* sir," the postman bowed holding his palms together as a sign of respect.

Parusuram smiled, "How are you Balayya?"

"I am fine sir, I got a telegram for you sir," he handed the telegram to him hesitantly.

Parusuram looked worried. He opened the telegram; he was shocked reading it, "Rama!" he exclaimed as if he lost his breath and he supported himself by standing against the rosewood door and the little bells on the door tinkled. The postman half expecting the outcome, held him, "Sir, is something wrong?" but he gulped his words when he heard Parusuram say, "Saraswathi!" and a tear escaped his eye.

Every tear has a story, and just that one tear of Parusuram made the postman freeze. With a blank face, Parusuram went in; he didn't know what to do. He saw his father who was now hugging Gita who had just completed her melodious chant. He could not think of an easy way of revealing the news. He could not think at all, he just blurted, "Dad, something terrible has happened!"

Pandit Vishwanath turned towards him, his face suddenly became grave, as if he knew what his son was about to say. He looked questioningly towards him.

"Father, Saraswathi is no more, she is dead." Parusuram's mouth was distorted; he never thought that such a day would come that he would tell his own father about the death of his own SISTER."

In an angry tone, Pandit Vishwanath shouted, "Are you in your senses? There must be some wrong information. Who told you……?" Pandit Vishwanath stopped when Parusuram put the telegram in his hand and slipped down, sitting at the base of the chair that he was sitting.

Pandit Vishwanath looked at the telegram; he could not believe his eyes. The telegram read, "Saraswathi and Gautam died in crash, Ishwak will be sent to his grandfather's house in a week."

Then he realised at the same time that someone by his side had stopped breathing; he quickly looked up to see Parvathi, her eyes reddened with a look of disbelief, pleading him to tell her it was all a big mistake. But his eyes could not lie. Without even a word born out of his mouth, Parvathi understood what he said. She could not bear the pain; she just collapsed and exploded into silent sobs, because the lady of the house was not supposed to cry out loud. Deependra took hold of his mother and Achyuta embraced his elder brother. Pandit Vishwanath just went inside the prayer room and sat before Goddess Durga like a kid with a problem running to a mother. He sat in front of the Great Mother and meditated, but he could no longer meditate; tears for the first time found their way into the great Pandit's eyes.

The postman witnessing the heartbreaking scene, left Tulasimandiram that was just a moment ago bursting with laughter and spiritual energy. Words cannot express an atmosphere of a mourning family, but anyone who had witnessed a death in the family can still hear the heart wrenching cries of the loved ones for the departed one.

New Home, New Friends

ISHWAK STEPPED DOWN the train's iron ladder with a faint fear in his eyes. He had a blue power ranger's backpack. He looked at the station, and every part of the station was clean. Unlike the Hyderabad railway station he had seen, it was a very small station with just one platform. Everything felt new, there were no towering buildings, there were no loud announcements on the speakers up above his head, only what appeared to be the remains of the speakers; there were no loud noises of traffic, the only loudest noise seemed to be that of the hollering train, which had now started off. But he recognised a faint scent that reminded him of his home; it's the sweet smell of the first rain quenching the thirst of sun burnt earth. Though there was no rain, the smell made it evident that rain had just stopped.

The station was nearly empty; only few people had boarded the train with their chicken baskets and potato sacks, and fewer people had got down the train. It seemed the people vanished with the train. Except for a sleeping pointsman in a cement cylinder-like shed across the track, no one was there. So he thought; but he felt a pull, a force near him. He looked around. He was alone except for his dad's friend. He felt scared. He always would sit next to his dad when he felt scared, and that reminded him of his father, and a flash of his father's open eyes looking at him, that were drenched with blood, came to him. He jerked to shove off the picture. He wanted to cry, but his throat stuck. He heard a voice, "You killed them Ishwak……why cry now?" He just stared.

Gautam's friend gazed at Ishwak with concern on his brow, 'How will he survive in this village after living in the ever-changing city of Hyderabad?' He sighed. He looked around and saw no one. He took out a slip from his pocket. He was supposed to come here, have they changed their minds. Would Saraswathi's father be still angry with her after all these years? Is he so cold hearted that he would not take his own grandson home? If he does not take Ishwak home, then I should make arrangements for adoption; he can stay with us for sometime and ……," as he was lost in his thoughts, a middle-aged man in a crisp white *panchi* (a large cotton cloth is folded into pleats and worn as the Indian trousers) and a white cotton shirt came into the station. He had three sandal wood lines drawn on his forehead with fingers. He looked at Ishwak, 'he is just like my dear Saraswathi,' his heart pounded with guilt.

Ishwak too stared at him, he was amazed looking at his uncle; he looked like his mother! That realisation again gave a flash and memories flooded into him – memories that showed his uncle was much younger and happier and taking care of him. He again waved off his head as if to push away these flashes, he did not understand why he was getting all these flashes. When he was successful in doing so, he realised that his uncle was standing in front of him and was talking to his dad's friend. He heard him say to his uncle, "You and Saraswathi, you are both so alike. People can easily take Ishwak to be your son!" For this Parusuram laughed who had already introduced himself to Gautam's friend, Shashi. Then he took a deep breath and looked down and saw Ishwak staring at him with his big brown eyes that were so familiar to him. He kneeled down before Ishwak, their eyes met each others. Ishwak also felt he was looking at those familiar eyes, which reminded of his mother, he felt his heart burst and he wanted to cry, and yet he was not able to cry. Parusuram wanted to say something, but not even a sound escaped his mouth.

Seeing that both the dearest people of Saraswathi lacked words, Shashi put his hand on Ishwak and turned to Parusuram and said in a lowered tone, "He is still in shock; he has not spoken a single word from that day." Parusuram could feel the boy's pain, he had talked to Shashi before and he said that Ishwak had witnessed his parent's death. He prayed to the Goddess, 'Oh Durgamma, no one should ever face such a situation' and he hugged the little boy. At first the boy was surprised and then there was a familiar scent on his uncle that reminded him of his mother, he felt secure again after a long time, he hugged his uncle too. Both seemed relieved; they found each other.

Shashi looked at them and made himself sure that there was nothing to be worried about. "Ok then, I have given your nephew to you safely; I should go now, the next train is in an hour, I will board the train and go. I will wait here in a waiting hall or something, err.......where is the waiting hall?" He looked around and as far as he could, but there was none at sight.

For this Parusuram turned and stood up, holding the boy's shoulder, "Shashi *garu* there is no waiting hall here; and it is considered bad manners to let a guest go away without visiting our home, please come with us and stay in our house at least for a day. We have made all the arrangements for you." He requested in a very delightful traditional manner with a classic Telugu accent.

Shashi excused himself that there were very few trains to go home and that he had a lot of work, but the gentle-mannered Parusuram was so firm that he finally won and he agreed to stay for one day. He thought he could be surer of Ishwak's future home and people around. Also, he had never stayed in a village before, and which he had always heard, was supposed to be very beautiful and pure.

They all put on their bags and came out of the railway station, the front yard of the railway station was like a twist in the story; as they came out, there was nothing in front of the station, not even one shop was seen on the premises and there was just one plain road, which looked like a national highway. There was a huge banyan tree with a large stone slab put around its trunk and a man was sleeping below the tree in a shaded place over the slab. It was dead calm out there, and that too, this time of the day at noon. Ishwak just stared at the banyan tree. There was only one *Tanga*, a local horse carriage, to which was tied an impatient horse and an equally impatient driver sitting on the driver's seat and scratching his ear. When the driver saw Parusuram his body language morphed immediately into one of a humble servant. He took their bags and put them on the wooden mesh below the soft cushions of the passenger seats. He then went to Ishwak and tried to take his backpack. To everyone's surprise, Ishwak just turned away facing the driver and started punching the driver's hand who withdrew and stood a few feet away. Shashi took hold of the boy and calmed him down. Both the men looked at each other, puzzled. But they did not take the fact very seriously because it was a new environment for the boy.

Ishwak looked around this new place, where now his new home would be. He did not see any tar roads here, there was mud everywhere. There was hardly any house for miles together. The land was blazing even more than he could imagine. But there were great old trees on either side of the road and he did not feel the heat. The great banyan tree spread its branch-like roots around itself. The tree stood tall with dignity, with magnificent grace; "Ficus benghalensis" the boy shouted out with joy. He had never seen such an old tree before. All the trees he had seen in Hyderabad had no such roots hanging down. He looked at his uncle, who was looking at him awestruck.

"What a clever boy you are! At such a young age how did you know the botanical name of banyan tree? Even I forgot the name myself; of course I read it when I was in intermediate after my 10th class. I am impressed!" Shashi was happy that the boy had spoken after a long time. He thanked God that the boy was recouping after the incident and he thought that the village's clean atmosphere was already having a good effect on him.

Ishwak too was surprised, 'How did I know the name?' He thought about it, it just came as a flash to him as if he had seen it long time ago. He also had the feeling that he had seen that same tree a lot of years ago. And somehow he wished the tree was yellow instead of dark green leaves, he felt that yellow leaves with its red fruit in the blazing sun would look more beautiful, "I wish the leaves were yellow, uncle."

At this, Parusuram who was nearly climbing the wooden step of the *Tanga* was taken aback. He turned around to see his nephew. 'Saraswathi had always said that!' It was as if Ishwak was just another form of his sister all over again. He walked towards him and placed his arm on his shoulder, "You know your mother always used to say that. You are just like your mother," and he smiled. But the boy just looked back at him with an expressionless face. The joy on the boy's face just a minute ago, faded away. Ishwak nodded and as the two men climbed up the Tanga, he climbed the stone slabs laid around the tree and touched the main branch of the tree at the base and then hugged it. His uncles could see that even after stretching his hand, he could only cover one-fourth portion of the tree trunk. Both of them inadvertently smiled, they both watched him climb down the steps. He slowly walked to the Tanga and sat between his uncles, carefully placing his backpack on his lap. The little anklet-bells tinkled as the horse ran, both the men were talking, Ishwak with an Eagle's vision could see the leaves on the highest tip of the tree turning yellow and he just watched them. As the noisy Tanga went away, there was a kind of silence in the air. The sparrows were not chirping; the eagles were not gliding in the air with their usual kingly pace, as if some invisible force was sucking out all the life force from that place. The great banyan tree was now shedding its yellow leaves slowly.

FROM THE KITCHEN of Tulasimandiram, a mixture of tingling aroma of the richest variety of food and snacks made everyone impatient to wait for the guest coming home. The children were peeking through the door looking at their mothers, aunts, and grandmother working busy as bees, working out their miracles in the kitchen. Once or twice they tried to steal a few hot sweets, but their grandmother was too cunning for them. As the children sat on the platform near the Peetam, devising new plans to steal the snacks, Pandit Vishwanath was lost in his thoughts as he lied down on his chair in the verandah shaded by the sweet-scented creeper. He had mixed feelings. Life seemed to have changed ten fold these last few days. HIS daughter……she was so intelligent! Her name suited her perfectly. She knew the Vedas as good as him and she also went along with the changing world and learnt the white man's language and was good at it. He remembered the day when his heart was bursting with pride the day when she got a scholarship for MBBS and she was going to become a doctor.

How he told everyone that his daughter would return to the village and treat everyone's problems. She even completed her MD in the next two years without being any burden to him. She was a jewel that Goddess Saraswathi had presented him. And one day, when he had found a suitable man for her, she refused to marry him. She talked about wanting to marry another man who she loved. BETRAYAL! ...He still felt the pangs dig into his heart and then he realised she was no more. How he had tried to chide her, make her understand not to marry a man below their caste, if only she had listened to him; he believed in the caste system and its implications of upper and lower caste, like many Indians who had failed to change according to the changing world.

His daughter answered, "God is in all of us equally, *nannagaru*. Only we have made these demarcations and condemn some people. Caste does not make a man, only his character makes a man."

Then he realised he could not change his daughter's opinion. In a cold tone that even now had astonished him, he looked into his daughter's eyes, "Get out of my house" and he looked away.

"*Nannagaru!*" tears rolled out of his precious daughter's eyes. But she stopped when she saw her father's firm mouth and stern face. She knew him; once he had said his word, he meant what he said.

All the members in the family were stunned to say anything. They never spoke against their great father and Parvathi was a shadow for her husband, she kept mum with tears rolling down her eyes and her sari *pallu* to her mouth to stop even an escaping sob.

That memory was still fresh in his mind. It was the day when for the first time he felt he was insulted, and then that memory was overlapped by the frame of the telegram arrival that read the lethal words of HER death – and now it didn't matter.

He waited for 'the boy' he thought. Then he had to remind himself 'my grandson' and looked impatiently at the Iron Gate on the other end of the garden. He sat in the easy chair made of rosewood and pretended to chant Durgamma's name, but today he was not. All sorts of questions rose in his mind, 'Does he look like his mother? Did he get his mother's intelligence? Poor boy, is he coping up well? What should I do?' And a question that came to his mind froze him, 'What if he asks why I didn't visit him all these years? What will I say to him? Will he ask if I hate his father?'

Just then his wife came with a glass of curd milk for him. He looked up at her. Today was the first time she was looking happy in the last few days and was actively cooking up all the special recipes and suddenly he realised how thankful he was to God for bringing her into his life. All these past few days, he was so consumed in his own grief that he did not even hold her hand to console her. As she put the glass down on the small wooden stool by his side and was about to leave, he caught her hand gently. Parvathi was surprised and turned with a questioning glance and when she saw his face filled with concern, she understood all that was unsaid. She simply smiled and put her free hand over his hand and they held their hands just for that extra minute which meant promises were being exchanged.

Just then there was a soft squeaking of the iron door at the other end of the garden. Smoothly letting go off each others' hands, the couple looked at the boy coming along the stone path, looking at the flowers and butterflies around him. Parvathi hurried into the home, while Pandit Vishwanath froze there looking at him, 'He just looks like her!'

Parusuram brought the boy to him and stood by his father, "This is Ishwak *nannagaru*," and turning to the boy he said, "This is your grandfather, your mother's father."

Both the grandfather and the grandson looked at each other, unsure what to do; when Shashi trying to break the ice introduced himself to the diffident grandfather, "Sir, I am Shashi, Gautam and Saraswathi's common friend. We were all together in college." So saying he turned to Ishwak, "Ishwak, ask for your grandfather's blessings son." To this, Ishwak set his backpack aside and bowed down to touch his feet and the Pandit who was not expecting a city boy to know all that, was amazed and suddenly kneeled down to hug the boy, "no need for that son – no need." A tear hid itself in the corner of his eye; all he could think of was Saraswathi – his precious daughter. All he could think, 'How foolish I have been to not accept my son-in-law and stayed away from my daughter and grandson?' When they stood up again, Ishwak's eyes showed no sign of any emotion. He was as dull and pale.

Ishwak had the same feelings of recognising this old man, but he had a memory of a much younger man reciting chants and meditating. He also had flashes of his cold face and it tormented him while he was hugging his grandfather. Like a tide of waves washing the lines on the sand, something cleansed those memories away and he just became quite. He didn't know what was happening to him and no one was there to talk to him. Now he was in this new place filled with expectant, familiar faces and he didn't know whom to trust, whom not to. Where were all these people when his Mom and Dad were there? But, once his mother had mentioned that his grandfather lived very far away and was too busy to come to their house. "We will go there once," she had said. And the words, 'we will go there once" echoed in his mind. Just then he saw a lady bringing a steel plate with a burning flame on it. He was scared.

Parvathi lit the camphor which she placed in the *aarti* plate with kumkum to invite her grandson home; it was a ritual which was done to drive away evil and bad luck from that person to whom the aarti was given. As she approached the boy, she saw the boy screaming and running away to hide behind Shashi and grabbed him so hard that Shashi nearly fell. He caught the pillar that was by his side. Guessing what might be the problem, Shashi signed to them to take away the aarti plate. Parvathi took the plate away and returned back and looked at him as if asking for forgiveness. Everyone felt, the reason he reacted that way was that he saw his parents' car explode into flames. Ishwak now came out of his hiding and looked at his grandmother, the same old feelings of already knowing her came over him, but there were some children of his age standing behind his grandmother; he felt glad to have no memory or familiarity with them. Then a girl in between all the boys came forward, "Would you like to see our room?"

Ishwak took this chance and looked at Shashi for confirmation, Shashi nodded, "Go on." He ran away, taking his backpack, with the rest of the bunch, slightly aware of his grandmother's disappointment, for she waited for thirteen years to hold him in her arms.

PARUSURAM LOOKED AT Ishwak playing with the kids. These three months went away like a sweet whiff. Parvathi was showering all her affection on him to make up for the lost time and everyone in the family took extra care for him so that he could cope with his sorrow. Even the children found him amusing; for he knew a lot of things they did not know, about his city, school, and video games that he had brought with him. Sometimes they would fight over the games, even with Ishwak. Gita would give them a sharp scolding and made them come back to their senses. This was one of those times and he laughed when Gita was showing them who the boss was. Ishwak himself had become close to Gita very much and Siddharth was his best friend. He knew cousins were the best of friends when they become friends. He was glad that Ishwak was laughing more these days and that blank expression he once had, was now very rarely found. He had become the prince of the house, much to the dismay of his eldest son, Phani who bossed the children saying he was the eldest. His son unlike himself, was very bossy than being responsible. But Parusuram knew that he was just in his teen years and he would slowly evolve to become responsible. Ishwak was also settling well in school because his syllabus was far more advanced than his peers' syllabus and he now turned out to be the best student in the school. He asked a whole lot of complicated questions to his teachers on purpose and made them a laughing stock, which made him very popular among students and he conducted plays and programs in the school, which even the teachers agreed were very professional. Parusuram was sometimes concerned about the quality of education he was receiving here, but then he remembered his sister, she had read in the same school, and she had done very well in her life and thus he was happy he was getting very well adjusted in this small village.

It was a Sunday and Ishwak saw that Gita was sitting near the Peetam and chanting some slokas from Bhagawad Gita.

Avinasi tu tad viddhi
Yena sarvam idam tatam
Vinasam avyayasyasya
Na kascit kartum arhati...

Ishwak did not understand what that meant. He knew it was Sanskrit, but he only knew rudimentary Sanskrit that his mother had forced him to learn, but he had always asked his mother what was the use of learning it. No one spoke Sanskrit nowadays and these days, it's Hindi, French, or Italian that was of any importance in their school. He was sure Gita did not know the meaning of slokas and somehow she had by-hearted them so well that she was chanting them. So with an intention to tease her, he went to her, "Gita, you chant so many slokas every day and everyone think you are a great intellect and all, but do you really know the meaning of those slokas?" he asked her in a sarcastic tone.

Gita, who was now much offended by the way he was asking the questions, said "I need not prove anything to you. My grandfather knows how well versed I am in the Gita and only people with knowledge of such things can ask me those questions. Ahem!" She snorted with disagreement and was about to leave, to sit in the garden to practice.

Ishwak started teasing her again, "Run mouse run! A very nice camouflage for things you don't know." And he started laughing and was going away.

"Wait! How dare you question my understanding on Gita? Ok, this once I will explain it to you. This sloka signifies the greatness and real nature of one's soul.

That which fills the body is indestructible. No one is able to destroy that imperishable soul.

It means every body has an individual soul, and the evidence of soul's presence is perceived as individual consciousness. I hope you understand what it means. Grandfather tells me what every verse in the Gita means. Isn't it great?"

Ishwak was astonished at that saying and though he did not grasp the full meaning of the lines, he wanted to learn more of the book. He felt sorry and said so to Gita for suspecting her understanding and to make it up for her; he left Gita there and went into the garden. He saw all the flowers there and plucked white roses and bunched them together and then he took out the red dense-petal hibiscus and arranged them outside the central roses. He added a few leaves here and there and he prepared a bouquet. He took it to Gita and gave it to her.

"For me!" Ishwak nodded smilingly. "Oh! Thank you so much. This is really beautiful.." She smelt the flowers and since then they had become so close that they could not be kept apart. Except for the time when Ishwak and Siddarth slept in the guest room that was closed before (now the room was opened as it was Saraswathi's room before she left the house), Ishwak and Gita walked together along the road to their school, which was a kilometre away, through the mango groves. Though they studied in different grades, they often met in the breaks, and while coming home and playing in the garden, everywhere they stayed together.

Seeing how close both the children had become, once or twice Gita's mother Kavita commented to Achyuta, "They both have become very close to each other, may be they will grow up and marry!" She spoke with girlish excitement. Achyuta was upset hearing it, "You have these old ideas filled up in your head. Cousins should not marry. There are some loopholes in our customs; it does not mean we follow them blindly. How come the children of two brothers or two sisters became siblings; and the children of a sister and a brother are eligible to marry? Even though Ishwak is my sister's son, and according to Hindu law they are eligible to marry, I still think they are cousins and cousins should not get married."

To this Kavita started mumbling in herself and started setting the bed sheet right. She thought, 'If Gita marries Ishwak she need not go to her in-laws' house, she can stay with us and she will not have any problems. But no! He would not understand, he does not want cousins marrying. God give this person some sense, after all, our ancestors might have thought of something and they might not be hundred per cent wrong. But what if both of them really want to marry each other? Then my husband can do nothing. Wow! That's a plan.'

As if Achyuta knew what was going on in her mind, he warned her gently, "Now don't go on putting any ideas into those children. They are kids and if you say to either of them that they will grow up to get married, they will have their fates written in their blank minds. The rest is up to you."

That made Kavita realise that what Achyuta said was true, it would be like forcing the children. So she let go off that idea.

But Phani who heard only a part of their conversation began teasing, "Ishwak, after a few years, you will send this invitation to every one." So saying he put a piece of paper in his hand.

"What is it?" Ishwak opened the paper.

MS. GITA weds MR. ISHWAK
YOU ALL ARE INVITED TO TULASIMANDIRAM

Ishwak became angry at once and shouted at him, "What nonsense is this? I am not going to marry Gita!" He threw the paper down.

But Phani was having too much fun looking at his face which had turned red with anger. He could not stop, "Mr. & Mrs. Ishwak...Mr. & Mrs. Ishwak... Mr. & Mrs. Ishwak!"

Hearing the commotion, Gita had come into the room and Phani stopped teasing Ishwak.

Gita picked up the paper and saw what was written on it and instantly became angry, "Who wrote this?" She questioned in her bossy voice. Everyone fell silent because having a fight with Gita would be to pick up a fight with grandfather and no one dared it. She looked at Phani who looked at Ishwak. She then turned to Ishwak and went to him, "Did you write this?"

Ishwak did not know what to do, he could not telltale on Phani, though he did not like it very much, it was just a prank, "Gita...don't be mad!"

Gita was taken aback; she thought Ishwak wrote it, "I didn't expect this from you Ishwak. I thought you were my friend. Why did you do this? You boys are all the same. Don't ever talk to me Ishwak. I wish I never had to see you. Go away from here!" So saying, she ran away to her mother.

When Phani saw that Gita left crying, he laughed, "That serves the little brat right."

The way Gita told him not to talk to her again somehow made him all alone again. A dark shroud fell on him and he once again had that blank stare in his eyes. He turned back and saw Phani giggling. He could not remember who he was or why he was laughing, all he could think of was to make him stop laughing and keep him quiet. He came near him and put both of his hands on his mouth so strong that Phani was scared. He struggled to put Ishwak away from him, but Ishwak was very strong for him. When he punched him, it was hurting him as if he was punching a wall. Now he was suffocating, he was not able to breathe or even to say a single word. All the other boys there were shocked to see Ishwak and did not realise what was happening. Siddharth then saw that his brother was really suffocating and tried stopping Ishwak by pulling his hands away from his brother, but Ishwak was too strong for him. He could not even push Ishwak away, he shouted at Aditya and Vikas for help and they all tried pulling him back, but they could not. Phani was already feeling dizzy when Siddharth shouted at Ishwak, "ISHWAK YOU ARE KILLING PHANI, HE IS YOUR BROTHER! CALM DOWN."

Ishwak heard this and suddenly a memory of his mother and father dying flashed before him and he stopped. Both Phani and Ishwak collapsed on the floor. Both of them were breathing deeply. Phani who now regained his composure, took an aim at his chest and punched him and looked at him scornfully, "It was just a prank, I don't know why you reacted the way you did. This punch serves you right, not that it will hurt you. You seem to have a lot of strength…" Phani stared in disbelief as Ishwak coughed up blood and twisted with immense pain.

Siddharth was also surprised that the punch actually hurt Ishwak. He rushed for his help, "What's wrong with you people today?" He saw the blood, "Aditya, bring a wet towel." Aditya and Vikas who were both just ten, did not understand why all this was happening and why the brothers were fighting with each other. Aditya ran and brought back a wet towel from the corridor and handed it over to Siddharth. Siddharth starting wiping off the blood, mumbling what fools they were and how they were fighting with each other.

Phani did not know what to do, 'He is my little brother, I should not have punched him. But what was that a moment ago? I punched him and he did not even budge. It's strange.' He saw Ishwak still bleeding and felt sorry for him and then he went to his side, sat beside him and spoke in an apologetic tone, "Ishwak, I am sorry." He did not wait for his response and he went away.

It was the middle of the day on a Sunday and everyone was resting and no one heard the fight. After nursing him, Siddharth went away leaving him alone. He did not know what to do after seeing this strange side of Ishwak. He went to his brother and sat beside him asking him if he was feeling fine. Aditya and Vikas who were by now scared of Ishwak also went away and sat with their big brothers.

Ishwak had never felt so lonely. He felt sure that all the brothers were sitting together, talking against him. He was not able to become close to any of the adults in the family. He had too many of the hidden memories of them in his mind. He had never seen them and yet he knew about everyone as if he had lived with them for a long time. Thus he avoided all the adults so that these memories would not bother him and he did not know why those memory flashes were actually there. Added to that, he had guilt – guilt of killing his parents. He could not talk about that with anyone. The only friends he had were Gita and Siddharth with whom he spent the day and they too seem to have been offended. Ishwak felt lost. It seemed no one needed him anymore.

Over the next few days, he became more and more quiet. He spoke less with Gita or Siddarth. After 2-3 days, Gita started talking to him, but he had become blank once more. Gita felt something was wrong. His eyes were always vacant, as if slowly Ishwak was losing something. He rarely smiled or laughed. Though Phani had forgotten all about the incident, Ishwak would not even talk to him. Ishwak started being alone. He went away for hours together into the forest on the small hills behind the mango groves. He would go away to the groves, sometimes even bunking school and whenever he was free after school. He was no longer popular in the class and he came home very late, ate food and slept in his mother's room. Siddharth tried to talk to him a few times, but as Ishwak was not at all speaking to him, he now slept along with his brothers in their old room.

Pandit Vishwanath who observed this particular change in Ishwak asked Parvathi what the reason could be. She also could not answer him. She and other people in the household had tried to be closer to him, but he did not like to talk to them. Parvathi stopped for a moment, "May be Ishwak does not like us because we sent his mother away!" Pandit Vishwanath became quiet for sometime. He took a deep breath, "May be subconsciously he felt his mother's pain. But these days he does not even talk to the kids. There is nothing much we can do but to pray to Durgamma to heal that boy's wounds."

No one knew what went on his mind. Ishwak was suffering, his memory flashes were becoming more intense; he now had flashes of his mother and father crashing into the tree as if he was in the car and he felt their pain. The last thing his mother said before dying, "Ishwak do not let that evil enter you." He did not know what his mother meant by that. He questioned himself again and again what that evil was. He found no answer. He had an overwhelming feeling of frustration; whenever he felt anger, he would go the forest near by, would try to find intuitively small animals, either rabbits or bandicoots and would catch them. Every time he tried to catch them, they burned up. A few escaped, but as the time went on, no creature survived his attacks. Even the plants and trees around the creatures dried up in an instant. His anger only quenched up when he had killed a few. He felt better and he would come home, feeling content and feeling surer of himself. He was feeling powerful as if no one could hurt him now. He was now able to subside the flashes.

One day, a few months after the incident with Phani, Ishwak returned home after his daily custom. A few elders of the village were sitting with his grandfather talking about a few mishaps happening in the town, which they felt like signs of a great calamity coming to the town. He went through the entrance and hid in the small passageway, listening to their words. He recognised the man now talking, to be one of the heads of the village Panchayat. The man had only white hair with bushy white moustaches that moved when he spoke, a lot of people in the village he observed had the big moustaches.

The old man was speaking, "......such an old tree, may be fifty to sixty years old, now it seems it has become lifeless."

Pandit Vishwanath did not understand, "Lifeless?"

"Yes Vishwanath *garu*, I saw it a few months ago, it was as green as a new rice field in rainy season, but now all its leaves have turned yellow!"

"Yellow! May be the tree is dying. May be it has reached the end of its life." Pandit Vishwanath spoke casually.

"No, the thing is that it still is very much alive, it still buds up leaves and fruits, just that it had turned yellow."

"Really! This is fantastic! How is that possible? But why do you think it is a sign of a calamity coming?"

"You may think it as silly Vishwanath *garu*, but the thing is that a few hunters who live in the forest over the hills, they say these days they are not able to catch any deer as they are hardly spotted and even rabbits have become rare. They say something made them so frightened that they ran away." Guessing Pandit Vishwanath's objection to it, he continued, "Though killing any living being is a sin according to the Vedas, it has to be accepted that a small tribe in our village depend on hunting for their food. It is what it is. We cannot change them. But the fact remains that the wild animals are running away. So I felt it was a warning."

"I agree with you, that nature has its own way of telling when a calamity is about to come. But what can I do Veeraiah?"

Ishwak suddenly became attentive when he heard what Veeraiah had to say, "Vishwanath *garu*, when I was a kid, my grandfather had told me about your great grandfather facing a problem something like this and that the then Zamindar had approached him to guide him in the proper way."

"Hmm...yes I remember now, please go on," Pandit Vishwanath knew there was a challenge ahead of him.

"You have great knowledge of *poojas* and *homas* to drive evil away and bring prosperity to the village. We will all be grateful if you can avoid any calamity that falls on us. This is a request from all the people in the village. These days even the crops also seem to fail even though there is plenty of water supply. We will help you in whatever way we can sir."

"I have to think about it. I have to know if these are random occurrences or some warning of a greater damage. I will surely look into it and perform the *yagna* that my great-grandfather had once done. I personally had never done it, but I will prepare myself," assured the pandit.

Thanking him profusely, all the village elders went away. Sensing who was behind the door, Pandit Vishwanath raised his tone, "Ishwak! What are you doing there?"

Ishwak composed himself and came in front of his grandfather. He stared at him. Pandit Vishwanath was puzzled to find that his eyes were very red as if he had not slept for days together and his iris had become darker than he had remembered seeing. Two black eyes were staring back at him and Pandit Vishwanath felt something was wrong. This alarmed him, "You should not eavesdrop when elders are talking, son."

"I wanted to know how your great-grandfather tackled the problem, can you tell me?" he still looked at him without blinking.

Feeling something was wrong with the boy, "I will tell you when the time comes son. Now go in and have your dinner. Where have you been going about? These days you are coming home too late."

"Just spending time in the mango groves." He looked displeased with the answer he got from the Pandit. He ran away into the house, he knew who else had the answer.

✧

GITA WAS SITTING in the backyard of the kitchen, on the little wooden plank tied up with jute rope to a large mango tree forming a swing. She was going through some of her slokas and learning them by heart, when suddenly she felt someone was staring at her; she turned around and gave a scream looking at two black eyes staring at her just by her side. Then she realised it was only Ishwak and scolded him, "Don't frighten me like that. It was not funny." But she was worried looking at Ishwak, he was not laughing and then she realised he was not joking. Irritated, she asked, "Why are you staring at me? What do you want?"

"Do you know our great-grandfather?"

"Yes, I know; he was a great man."

"Did you know he saved this village during his time from a big catastrophe?"

"Yes, and since then there has always been rainfall and plenty of crop in this village. No problems at all." Gita spoke as if she saved the village.

"Can you tell me what he did?"

"Why do you want to know?"

"I am curious, that is all!"

"Ok listen carefully. This happened a long time ago. Our great-grandfather had an elder brother. Though he was the eldest, our great-grandfather Pandit Siva Rama Krishna, was known to have the talent for Vedas and he was encouraged by his father to go deeper into the other magical books that he had. The elder brother took it as an insult and had gone away from the home for a few years. Some say that he might have gone in search of a powerful guru and some say he learnt things himself by sacrificing living beings. When he came back, Pandit Siva Rama Krishna knew just by the look in his eyes that he had become an egoistic who thought he had the power of God. But he thought he could change his brother after counselling him. As the days went by, the lakes in the village were drying up, the trees in the forests were dying, and a lot of animals were found dead. Someone close to the Zamindar had told him the reason for this and trusting the wisdom of Pandit Siva Rama Krishna, he told the truth to the great Pandit. His elder brother was performing some rituals in which he was consuming the life force of all the helpless creatures in the lake and the forest. He was becoming powerful because of this. Pandit Siva Rama Krishna had to confront his elder brother, which you know is very hard because elder brother was next to a father, and younger brothers never talked against their elder brothers. When confronted, the elder brother was so furious that he had used some kind of power over the younger one that it is said that it burned him. Then Pandit Siva Rama Krishna found that he had to stop his brother and hence he performed a *yagna*, a ritual so as to drive away the evil spirit that sought abode in his body. It was one of the complicated *yagnas*, where a number of wise pandits sit and do it for a whole day and there should be no interruption. But if the elder brother knew about this *yagna*, he would surely come to disrupt it; so Pandit Siva Rama Krishna arranged a Peetam that had special powers in it, to stop any kind of intrusion." At this, Gita felt excited, "ingenious, isn't it?"

"Yes yes, now go on with the story," hurried Ishwak completely missing the implication.

Annoyed with Ishwak's impatience, Gita crossed her hands tightly and refused to speak anymore.

"Ooh! Stop this childishness, tell me the rest Gita!" seeing that Gita was not speaking anymore, he relaxed and softened his tone, "Sorry Gita, now I will be patient enough, tell me now...please." He smiled.

"Now that's better. Where was I? Oh yes! When the Peetam was constructed, arrangements were made for the *yagna*. The Peetam was big enough for five pandits to sit (five pandits were very important to represent *pancha bhootalu* (the five components of nature). There was a *Homa Gundam* in the middle, where fire consumed the ghee that the pandits put while reading Vedic chants in praise of the Goddess Durga. A small golden box with an 'OM' symbol etched on it was placed and all the goodness coming out of the prayers was directed to it and it slowly transformed from a simple-looking gold box to a magical and powerful holder of any evil that came in the way of Pandit Siva Rama Krishna. As expected, the elder brother tried to stop the prayer, but he could not and then finally when it was all over, the evil spirit was sucked out of him and it entered the golden box. Everyone thought it was successful, but unfortunately there was no spirit left in the elder brother's body, so he died. Even though our great-grandfather was successful in saving the village, he could not save his own brother." Gita was so immersed in telling the story that she did not see Ishwak perspiring and that he was very restless. When she turned to face him she saw blood-shot eyes and it frightened her. She was even more scared when Ishwak suddenly caught her hand.

"What was the name of the elder brother?" Ishwak demanded.

"Name of the brother? Why? Why do you want to know?" Gita was trembling by now.

"Just tell me the name girl!" Ishwak nearly startled her.

"Name of the brother…hmmm…I don't remember Ishwak! You are scaring me, let me go, please let me go," Gita pleaded.

"Tell me the name, remember it. It's very important – tell me!" Ishwak pressured her more.

Gita tried to remember, but when she heard the story from her grandfather she was too involved in the technique and the little golden box that she did not remember his name, but she concentrated more and finally, "Oh! I remember it. It's Pandit Manishankar!" And suddenly the grasp loosened and she almost fell down. She looked up to see Ishwak and his eyes had completely become red and were filled with anger.

Ishwak saw the Peetam and he started laughing, "I have been waiting for this moment for a long time – a very long time." So saying, Ishwak ran towards the main gate and vanished into the route to the mango groves.

It seemed to Gita as if he was half mad. But she did not tell this incident to anyone thinking Ishwak might get into trouble, but Pandit Vishwanath saw everything that had happened from the kitchen door while he was standing in a shaded place; so neither of them had seen him. Parvathi who saw the Pandit stand there for such long time knew something was wrong and when she came to stand by his side, she only saw Gita studying. She smiled and went on with her work. She failed to see the deep furrow of concern and fear on the Pandit's brow. He went to the prayer room and removed a heavy iron case that was locked with a rusted lock. It had not been opened since a long time. It was time to refresh his memory.

The Curse

IT WAS A full moon day; the night light wrapped everyone in its charm. The red roof tiles of Tulasimandiram almost looked white as the moonlight dipped them in their magic. The night was extremely quiet, it had been a few days since the crickets created nuisance in the night. There were no bats flying or any owls watching over Tulasimandiram. The silence engulfed the place, except for an occasional dribbling of the water drops from the tap that fell on the brass vessels left under it. There was a silent creaking of the damaged fan in one of the rooms.

A nimble-footed man slowly walked through the garden shadows, hiding from the moonlight. He wrapped a cotton towel on his head and over his face, leaving only the eyes. He tied a dagger in its sheath across his chest. He slowly climbed the edges of the tiles, very careful not to disturb them. He climbed over the tiles to reach the middle part of the house, where an iron grill was placed covering the open area above the Peetam. He took out a small wire cutter and cut the iron grill so that he could squeeze himself down. He tied a rope to the grill and slowly climbed down just by the side of the Peetam, being careful not to land on it as if he respected it. He bowed to the Peetam and counted the rooms from the passageway and made sure it was the room he was looking for. He crawled up to that room and slowly opened the door. He looked at the boy sleeping on the bed, motionless just like the night. The man started breathing fast, his every step towards the boy was hesitant, but he had to push himself and when he stood by the bedside facing the boy, he removed the dagger from the sheath and held it high above the boy with his right hand. He put his left hand on the boy's mouth so that he would not scream. As he put his hand on the boy, he felt the boy was as cold as ice and was expecting him to wake up and scream, but the boy lay still. Taking a deep breath, he tried to stab the boy with his dagger, looking at the boy's closed eyelids.

Just when he was an inch near his chest, the boy suddenly opened his eyes and he was terrified to see that the whole of his eye ball was blood red and before he could stab the boy, a strong blow kicked him over to the wall next to the bed and he felt a sharp pain in his heart, the dagger was in him now, pinning him to the wall; half-expecting his fate, he smiled and as the pain jabbed his heart, he jerked to find the ground, which was a few inches below his feet. Wanting to alert the people in the house about this cursed child, he opened his mouth. Just then the boy read some verses that blocked his voice and he was dead. The boy sucked the spirit in him and smiled, just a few days more and he would become all powerful. Everything happened in a split second – a 'mere' second changes everything!

All the people heard a hard thud and woke up and came running to Ishwak's room. Pandit Vishwanath was shocked and stood there hesitantly, unsure what to do. Parvathi who was just behind him gave a scream. Instinctively, she ran in before Pandit Vishwanath could stop her and hugged the boy, closing his eyes with her palm. The boy froze with her touch as it reminded him of a motherly touch taking care of him. He calmed down and his eyes no longer looked red. She took him out of the room. The others reached there a little later, but Pandit Vishwanath asked Kavita and Shanti not to enter the room. He called his sons into the room and showed them what had happened. The body of the masked intruder now lied down, awry with the head resting on the wall. No one was able to make out how this man was killed or why he had come to this room. Pandit Vishwanath asked Achyuta to go to the police station and alert the police.

Even the kids woke up and saw their grandmother taking away Ishwak to her room and they watched her taking care of Ishwak, who had now slipped off into sleep as if nothing had happened. Gita was worried now. She was nearly on the right path of guessing, but she could not correlate two separate suspicions; so she brushed them away.

By the time the police came and took the dead body away, it was seven o'clock in the morning. The police were baffled with a murder case at their hands because Panipakam was a very peaceful village and the only cases that come to their hands is an occasional brawl between two drunkards. They did not even have records of someone killed in that area for decades together. All the reasons why he could have come to Tulasimandiram did not work out. There was nothing precious in the house except for a few gold jewels that the ladies wore, there were no electrical appliances except for a radio, or any art works present. Nothing valuable was there in the house. There were no enemies either, they thought. Everyone in the village respected the family and Pandit Vishwanath never interfered in anyone's life. Finally, after much investigation someone in the village recognised him to be a man from the tribe that lived in the forest at the outskirts of the village. But that was even more baffling. The tribe and the village had existed peacefully for a long time. They rarely ventured into the village, except for selling forest herbs or hand-made decorations. The police also could not believe that a boy of Ishwak's age could kill such a strong man double his height. The police thought that whatever reason he had come there, he might have slipped and fallen on his own dagger and it pierced him, but suspicion remained of the mark on the wall, high up, of its origin. The talk went about in the village for a few days, and like many things was forgotten and remained an exciting thing told to newcomers.

People in the village thought it was some kind of curse that followed the boy from the city and many were sure that the same curse was the reason behind his parent's death.

The room was locked up after it was cleansed with turmeric water and *Tulasi*. Everyone in Tulasimandiram even forgot that the room existed. The daily life of Tulasimandiram again started without any disruptions. Though Ishwak was reluctant, Parvathi did not listen to any word he said and always insisted on him to be with her. She did not allow him to wander off into the forest and even while going to the school, one of his uncles accompanied the kids. Gita studied Ishwak carefully. It had been some days since he had acted weirdly. He pretty much looked like the kid she met when he first came to their house. She was happy to get back her friend.

Ishwak observed Gita looking at him and smiled, Gita smiled back. He came near her, "Gita, please forgive me for hurting you the last few days. Can we be friends again?" He looked at her pleadingly.

Gita laughed, "Forgive you for what? We were friends always. What are cousins for?"

Ishwak gave a broad smile, "Cool! Hey I want to show you something wonderful, would you like to see it? It is in the forest just after the mango groves." Ishwak was excited.

"In the forest? But Ishwak, it's dangerous to go there!" Gita looked at him doubtfully.

"Oh no! It's not dangerous, I used to go there everyday; I never felt it was dangerous and you know something, there is an old temple of Goddess Kali. It is beautiful! You will love it. Besides, if we are in the temple, we are in the house of God, how can it be dangerous?" Ishwak asked innocently.

"Really! An old temple? I never knew it existed. I want to see it, but I don't think grandma would allow us to go there, that too after, you know what happened." Gita frowned.

"I know they will not allow us. That's why we will go in the night after everyone had slept." Ishwak spoke in a whispered tone.

"At night? Oh no! I won't come out at night. No way." Gita looked scared.

"I understand. No problem. I am also scared to go there, but the thing is when the last time I visited there, I left my mother's photograph there. I just want to get it back," sighed Ishwak.

"You have never talked about your mother before. I can understand how badly you want to get it back. Ok, we will just slip for a few minutes, take it back and come right away. We will be careful," Gita cheered up.

"You are a real friend. Yes, we will do just that. Thank you so much Gita," Ishwak was very happy. The time had come!

PANDIT VISHWANATH SAT up late, praying to his Durgamma. He has been practicing the particular slokas that his great-grandfather had practiced in the same place a very long time ago. He was grateful for the Peetam that his great-grandfather had constructed. The *Zamindar* who saw his power, had given the place surrounding the Peetam to him and ordered his own mason to construct a house according to *Vasthu Shastra*, a traditional study of building a house, and Pandit Siva Rama Krishna had asked the mason to construct the house in such a way that it surrounded the Peetam so that the future generations could live safely without any illness or poverty. The house was then named Tulasimandiram symbolising its powers of healing. No one except Pandit Vishwanath knew what trouble was brewing in this simple house.

After completing the prayer, he entered the room where all the boys slept, made sure Ishwak was sleeping and went to his own room and tossed in the bed by his wife's side, who was innocently sleeping after a tiring day of work. He put his palm on her head and thanked God once again for he has been the luckiest man in the world; he had a perfect wife who never complained, four kids who were intelligent and obedient, and grandchildren who were in every sense a blissful part of his life. Then he remembered *his* Saraswathi, he was so happy when she was born. He knew she was special right away and had taught her all that he knew at a very young age. He should not have sent her away like that with hatred in his heart. He did not hate her, he just hated her decision. He had felt many a time that the reason for her unnatural death was sending her away without his blessings and now her only son was at stake. He dozed off into sleep.

He felt he was in someone else's body. He was hiding from someone behind a tree. As he looked more clearly, he saw Ishwak firing something with his bare hands. He was killing rabbits and deer which came that way. He burnt the trees too. As he burned them, a red aura from the dead animals rose into the sky and he started sucking them up and he was laughing like a madman. Then he realised to whom the body belonged. It was the body of the man who tried to kill Ishwak. Now he understood why he tried to kill him.

Suddenly, Pandit Vishwanath was jolted again to an unfamiliar place of a school playground and as he walked barefooted in the hot sand of the ground, he saw his daughter. Though he knew it was a dream, his heart skipped a beat. Saraswathi smiled at him and pointed something to him. He looked right to where she pointed her finger and he saw Ishwak sitting under the blazing sun, digging something up and when he took out the shiny box, he felt a stab of pain in his heart for he knew his grandson only had a few days to live. His whole body felt numb and he was not able to move, he had to get away from the place before the seal of the little golden box was released; for the evil spirit would surely know he was here and try to infuse into his own spiritual energy, which was even more dangerous. He tried to move his feet, but he felt as if he was stuck in quick sand. He prayed to Durgamma to send him help, just then his daughter appeared by his side and held his hand. She spoke in a heavenly voice, "*Nannagaru*, please save my son, he is my life, an eternal part of me." Then suddenly, Saraswathi's form turned into an image of Gita and she pulled him out. As she pulled him out of the quicksand, she feebly said, "Help". Pandit Vishwanath woke up from this dream of revelation.

Discovering so many things in one dream, he did not know how to control his emotions; then he remembered the face of Gita pulling him away from the dream. He instantly knew Gita was in danger. He went to look for her in the kid's room, but she was not there and so was Ishwak. He had to protect her and somehow save Ishwak too. He did not know how? Manishankar had become very powerful by now!

The Sacrifice

"WOW! THIS TEMPLE is so beautiful. I always loved old temples of stone. This temple looks even more beautiful because of the creepers that have dug themselves deep into the stones as if trying to find the essence of God in these stones. Look even the creepers are paying their homage to Goddess Kali by blooming just at her feet. Amazing, Ishwak! Thanks for bringing me here. If you were not so convincing, I would never have come here. You are so brave." Gita was lost in her own observations.

Ishwak looked at her crying out for her to get away from here as soon as possible. He was trapped deep inside his own body with no way of getting out. The body was now too powerful for him, for it was filled with so many souls of all the living beings that Manishankar had killed. He tried to fight him off at start, but his own hatred, loneliness, and guilt had given Manishankar a place in his heart. Manishankar had manipulated him into believing all he had said. At the beginning, Manishankar did not know why he was in a golden box or why he craved for spiritual energy from other living creatures. Then one day when he heard the story of Pandit Siva Rama Krishna and his elder brother, Manishankar, he got back his memory and with it, his thirst for revenge. Since then, Ishwak could not fight him. Manishankar's energy doubled and tripled, and since then, he had been trying to destroy Ishwak's own soul. Ishwak, who now had given up, could only just cry and wish for others to get away from Manishankar. It was too late when he learnt that with each spirit, comes a set of memories which are unique for every creature, so when Manishankar killed his mother and father, his mother's memories always came back to him to tell him of the family's kindness and love. His mother's memories only meant to make him understand he was not alone, but he understood those flashes too late. Ishwak now sat in a corner of his mind and wished that someone could stop this monster Manishankar.

Just when he was about to give up, he understood the move of Manishankar that he was going to sacrifice Gita to Goddess Kali. Gita was the particular target because she knew the process of evoking the Peetam's power or subduing it. He could not let Manishankar kill Gita! He had to fight one last time. Just when Manishankar in the form of Ishwak was coming forward to kill Gita, Ishwak's soul fought him with all the will he had and shouted out aloud, "Gita run away! Manishankar is trying to kill you. Run away!" It took all his strength and will power, but soon Manishakar took over.

Gita who intuitively felt the dwelling of an evil spirit, but was not sure of it, now understood why Ishwak was acting the way he did. She started to runaway, when she felt a blow on her head with a wooden plank. She fell down forward and turned on her back. Everything felt blurred and she could feel something warm and sticky flowing through her ear. She saw Ishwak looking down on her. Somehow she mustered all her strength and spoke out:

Avinasi tu tad viddhi
Yena sarvam idam tatam
Vinasam avyayasyasya
Na kascit kartum arhati

"Remember it Ishwak!" and she fell unconscious.

Ishwak felt he had heard that sloka somewhere. Then he remembered Gita saying in her I-know-everything tone, "*That which fills the body is indestructible. No one is able to destroy that imperishable soul.*" Ishwak then understood, 'I am indestructible.

Even the strong Manishankar cannot destroy me! He realised that if he gave up, he would kill everyone in his family just to get revenge on someone who was long gone. Just like the fight of conscience with selfishness in every person's daily life, Ishwak's soul fought with Manishankar's spirit, both of which were trapped in the same body.

Just then Pandit Vishwanath came to the crumbling temple and saw Ishwak staring ahead blankly in silence. He did not understand why he sat there like that, but then saw Gita lying down in a pool of blood. He carefully went to her and put his finger near the nose to see whether she was still breathing. He was overjoyed to feel she was breathing. He took out the cotton *kanduva*, a towel like cloth that is worn over the shoulder, and tied it around Gita's head, where he found the wound. He picked her up and carried her slowly towards his house. Rather than the hospital, he felt that the Peetam was the best place for Gita to be. As he hurried, Manishankar realised what had happened and he followed the trail of Pandit Vishwanath.

He shouted out loudly in a hoarse voice to let the Pandit know he was coming to take away his granddaughter. Manishankar was still being pestered by Ishwak, but he was too strong a spirit for the boy and he still had control over Ishwak's body. Manishankar saw that Pandit Vishwanath was nearly near the gate of Tulasimandiram, but now he was confident that he was powerful and there still was time for the Peetam to be evoked.

Pandit Vishwanath called out to everyone in the house as he lay down Gita on the Peetam. He tried to think fast, he needed four more pandits who knew the *slokas*. He picked Achyuta, Deependra, Phani and Siddharth. But he was worried because Siddharth only knew half of the *slokas*. Just as he started practicing for the *yagna* on Peetam, he chose Gita instead of Siddharth and he thought they would do fine, but he did not expect this turn of events. But right now he had no choice. He only hoped it would work out. As soon as she was laid down on it, her bleeding stopped and she looked peaceful as if she was sleeping. The Pandit asked his son

Parusuram to put the *kumkum* and turmeric mix while chanting the name of Durgamma. Parusuram did not ask any question and went into the Prayer room to get it. Just then Kavita and Parvathi came out of their rooms and saw their daughter lying down on the Peetam and they were confused as to what happened to her and as they went towards her to touch her, Pandit Vishwanath who was sitting beside the unconscious Gita, stopped them, "You cannot touch her now. I have started the process of activating the Peetam and till such time as the *yagna* completes, no one can come in or come out of the circle. Do not worry Kavita. She will be all right. I will give my life to *Yama* (the God of death) before he takes her life away."

Just then the front end of the house blew into pieces and Ishwak was standing there with his red eyes. "Hiding behind the Peetam I see. Pandit Vishwanath, you are just like your grandfather, hiding behind that Peetam of yours. My little brother caught me when I was weak, do you think you can do what he had done? You neither have the spiritual energy as my little brother had nor am I weak. Who is going to save you? The time is just right. I have got to get your souls, though not as strong as me – yours and Gita's. I will become powerful enough to do anything as I please and when I imbibe your souls, this Peetam cannot hurt me.

Parusuram who was drawing the line with powder of *kumkum* and *Pasupu* stopped on the opposite end of the Peetam where Ishwak stood. He was scared to move, but if the line was not completed, the Peetam would not start working. He took a deep breath and took hold of a fist full of the mixture and started hurrying along the final side of the rectangular Peetam. To everyone's horror, suddenly Ishwak saw him and with just a stroke of his finger, he sent flames which engulfed Parusuram and with his fist tightened up, he rolled over trying to extinguish the flames. Then finally when the flames extinguished, he felt burning pain all over the body. The pain immobilised him. He had no will to move and then a soft hand touched his fist containing the mixture and he felt it was Saraswathi who was nudging him to complete the line.

Manishankar who thought Parusuram was dead, started moving towards Gita to kill her and make her soul his own, and as he bent to take hold of her, a flash of pink light rose up from the line and became a shield, a barrier to protect the ones inside and burnt Ishwak's hand. Manishankar realised that Parusuram had completed the line before dying. In his disappointment, he roared out loud. He had waited all this time for that perfect moment when he could get his revenge and his eternal life only to be again sealed into a box. He had to think of a way fast. The Pandit had already started the *yagna* and due to the power of the Peetam, slowly Gita seemed to come into consciousness. He knew Siddharth would not stand up till the end of the yagna, but if Gita wakes up, she would surely add up to the strength and there would be no turning back.

Manishankar spoke out, "Pandit Vishwanath I will give you two choices, listen carefully." The Pandit did not heed any of his words. "I still have your grandson's body. If you complete the yagna, I will anyhow be sealed in a box for eternity, so before getting sealed up in a box, I will kill your grandson and also your family outside the Peetam."

Pandit Vishwanath knew this would come to that, but he had no choice. His daughter had asked him to save her son, but he had to complete the yagna or he could not imagine what he can do with the power of the Peetam. He had no choice, but to continue the yagna.

This irritated Manishankar. Suddenly Ishwak started jerking as if he was having a seizure, he coughed up blood. Ishwak was shivering profusely. Parvathi ran to the boy to help him in anyway she could, even though she knew anytime Manishankar can take hold of Ishwak and would kill her. She hugged him and prayed to Goddess Durga to help him and show them a way of saving this innocent boy. Ishwak felt the comfort and warmth of his mother in Parvathi. He did not see it all this time and now when he finally knew he had a mother, it was too late. But Ishwak knew that Manishankar would kill her, he had to fight. He saw Gita too. He fought with Manishankar tirelessly. But all the spirits Manishankar had devoured, acted as a boost to him and it felt like fighting a hundred people all at once. And suddenly, Ishwak's tongue was pulled into his throat and his eyes and nose were bleeding too. He quivered with pain. Ishwak could feel his veins burning as if the blood in his veins was boiling up. Parvathi touched his forehead and felt that he was burning up, she asked someone to bring some water, but as if the sun had scorched up the place, all the water in the house evaporated into thin air. Parvathi could not endure the little boy's pain, she called out to her husband, "Oh great Pandit Vishwanath, my soul mate, save this little boy's life, even if it meant sacrificing your life." She looked straight into his eyes and Pandit Vishwanath knew what she meant. Both of them knew they had no other choice. But if he sacrificed his life, there will be another member less on the Peetam; he did not know what to do. He tried to wake up Gita; she healed up totally, but had not yet become conscious. "Parvathi, do whatever you can, I need few more minutes."

Parvathi did not understand what she could do. All she could was to hug him tight and pray to Durga. She prayed to Goddess Durga continuously to help her boy and she meditated more and more. Slowly her consciousness left the mortal world and she felt she was near the feet of the Great Mother. Her body became a kind of shield to Ishwak and he started feeling better. He was not bleeding anymore. Even his seizures stopped.

Manishankar felt he was trapped in Ishwak's body. He tried everything possible to burn Ishwak's body from inside, but he could not. He calmed down. And with all the power he had, he concentrated on Parvathi to separate her and Ishwak. No one could see what happened, but Parvathi screamed, "Mother!" and she fell a few feet away. Kavita and Shanti were too scared to do anything and both of them hugged the kids in fear.

Pandit Vishwanath looked at the unconscious body of Parvathi. Tears that have been imprisoned for too long burst out flooding his eyes and he stammered in between the chanting of the slokas;

when Manishankar noticed the pause and Ishwak was now looking at the Pandit. Pandit Vishwanath composed himself and resumed his chanting. Just then he saw Gita opening her eyes. Pandit Vishwanath had never felt so happy in his life. He signalled Gita to wake up and chant the mantra he was reciting now. Gita who now was alert, looked at Ishwak and her grandmother, and started chanting. With a deep breath, Pandit Vishwanath stopped the chanting and kissed Gita on her forehead and bade farewell to the others sitting on the Peetam; still chanting slokas – terrified. Though there was no chance of asking any questions right now, all the five glared at him bewildered as to what he was doing. Pandit Vishwanath jumped out of the Peetam and he fell on the ground beside the elevated Peetam. Everyone looked with astonishment as the Pandit seemed to have aged at least ten years and he had cuts all over his body. But Gita did not let anyone stop chanting and motioned with the hand to concentrate more on the *Homa Gundam*, the fire burning in the middle. It was their only chance.

Manishankar was surprised to see Pandit Vishwanath daring to come out of the protected field, "Oh! You really love your wife, do you? But it was a fatal love. Now you are going to die!" Meekly, Pandit Vishwanath stood looking at his grandson, whose eyes looked helpless and his body moved to attack him. Ishwak moved his hands as if he was throwing a ball, but it was a faint yellow light of force and it hit Pandit Vishwanath and in one split second, the great Pandit took his last breath.

Everyone present there paused as if they were unsure it was a dream or not. Gita was about to get up when Achyuta, her father caught her hand and signalled her to sit. The chanting did not stop. Kavita and Shanti took the kids in to the room nearest to them. Parvathi and Parusuram lay on either side of the Peetam, motionless, breathing shallowly while Manishankar finally thought he had succeeded this time. He sucked the soul out of the Pandit as Ishwak opened his mouth.

Manishankar did not know why the five people inside the Peetam's shield were still chanting. To him, the game was over. Now he could pass the shield and no one could stop him. He now tried to memorise the sloka that would disintegrate the Peetam's energy; strangely, he could not! He tried and tried again, but could not. Slowly he began to feel weak and he realised his folly. Pandit Vishwanath's spirit was so strong that his spirit chose to infuse with Ishwak's spirit that was fighting all along diligently. The two spirits were infused, making Ishwak's spirit so strong that he fought powerfully and finally Manishankar was pushed away from Ishwak's body. Manishankar, who still could not believe what had happened, lurked above Ishwak trying to figure out the next step when Ishwak took out his backpack from his back and removed the golden box. Before Manishankar could realise what was pulling him, the golden box pulled him in fiercely and shut itself tight.

"I did it Gita!

Avinasi tu tad viddhi
Yena sarvam idam tatam
Vinasam avyayasyasya
*Na kascit kartum arhat*i

No one can destroy my soul." And Ishwak collapsed unconscious.

ISHWAK OPENED HIS eyes to find his aunt, Shanti nursing him who was smiling on him, "How are you feeling son?"

He felt his head hurt and all his body sore, but he had not felt this good for a long time now, "A lot better Shanti *pinni.*" Then with a skipped heartbeat, he remembered the horrible night when he killed his own uncle, his grandmother who tried to save him, and his grandfather. He felt guilty more than ever. His heart burst out with grief, and he started crying out loud.

Sensing his sorrow, Shanti rubbed his back, "Don't worry son, everything will be alright. It was not your intention, that cowardly Manishankar baited you and used you. We all know that son. Don't cry!"

"But I was not strong enough *pinni.* I killed all the people who loved me so much." He still wept.

"All the people who loved you! But we are still here." A familiar, old and gentle voice spoke to him.

Ishwak rubbed his watery eyes and he saw, "Grandma!" And as she came towards him he jumped up and hugged her. "I thought you were dead Grandma!" Then he looked at her forehead, she had not kept the big round bindi that she always so fondly applied with *kumkum* and wore a plain white sari, which meant that his grandfather was no more. His heart crashed.

"What happened my child?" Parvathi looked at him worried.

"I am sorry about Grandfather." He took a deep breath.

"Oh! But his spirit still dwells in you." She smiled.

"And uncle Parusuram? Where is he?" Ishwak asked almost hesitantly.

"You talking about me son?" A booming voice behind his grandmother came out.

Ishwak was blissfully surprised and looked beyond Parvathi and from the door, Parusuram walked in with a slight limp and a casted hand. He jumped out of his bed and hugged his uncle, "I am so happy to see you Uncle."

Parusuram took his support and sat on the bed holding his hand, "You cannot imagine how happy I am, son. I was worried these three days when you were sleeping still, but just looking at you smiling makes me feel I am looking at my sister."

"Really!" Ishwak blushed.

"Yes and did you know, me and Saraswathi were the best of friends and we were always together when we were kids. We can also be very good friends. Is that ok?" Parusuram smiled.

"Friends? Hmm…I have a better idea. I will call you Dad!" Ishwak looked at him expectantly.

Parusuram's eyes glistened, "Perfect!"

Everyone started laughing and just then the rest of the family joined and Gita stood there, looking with an I-saved-your-life attitude in silence.

"Oh! Alright. You know everything and yes, you saved my life," Ishwak spoke uninterestedly.

"What! Is that the way you thank me?' Gita was irritated.

Ishwak smiled and took Gita's hand, "I am sorry! I really owe you one Gita. Thanks for everything. I don't know what would have happened if you were not there." Ishwak looked very humble and thankful.

Gita smiled shyly, "You cannot credit it entirely to me. Everyone helped that day. Even Siddharth for the first time in his life, remembered all the slokas from start to the end you know."

Siddharth disgusted with this teasing, even after remembering all the slokas, "hey, when will you stop acting like a snob? When required, I know what to do." And all the cousins put their hands on his head and rubbed it to tease him more and everyone ran away into the garden to play.

Parvathi went to their room and stood looking at Pandit Vishwanath's photo hanging on the wall, looking at him silently; asking him why he left her here when he himself was with Durga. Just then Ishwak came to her room and took her hand, "during that night, when you did not care what a danger I was to you and hugged me, I became stronger Grandma. I felt I was with my mother again" and he hugged her again.

Parvathi thanked her husband for what he had done. With serene look in her eyes, she pushed back the small hair tips falling on his forehead and kissed him there, just like she kissed her long-lost daughter.